The
TAPESTRY
Makers

Il y a un autre monde mais il est dans celui-ci
Paul Éluard

The Tapestry Makers

First Edition published 2025 by Bunny Publishing.

bunnypublishinguk@gmail.com

Copyright © Rhiannon Jenkins Tsang 2025

The right of Rhiannon Jenkins Tsang to be identified as the author of this work has been asserted by her in accordance with the Copyright, Designs and Patents Act 1988

All rights reserved. This book is sold subject to the condition that no part of this book is to be reproduced, in any shape or form. Or by way of trade, stored in a retrieval system or transmitted in any form or by any means, electronic, mechanical, photocopying, recording, be lent, re-sold, hired out or otherwise circulated in any form of binding or cover other than that in which it is published and without a similar condition, including this condition being imposed on the subsequent purchaser, without prior permission of the copyright holder.

This is a work of fiction and any resemblance to any person living or dead is purely coincidental.

Cover Design by Charlotte Mouncey

Printed in Great Britain by Ingram Sparks

A CIP catalogue record for this book is available from the British Library

ISBN 978-1-8381508-2-2

The TAPESTRY Makers

RHIANNON JENKINS TSANG

BUNNY PUBLISHING

> To Jean
> love from
> Rhiannon

For my Father

PROLOGUE: THE TAPESTRY TEACHER

No one notices me, the old spinster. That's their mistake. I've spent most of my life hidden behind a loom. It's safe there. Look at my face: grey, half in shadow, reflected in a weaver's mirror! I was never a great beauty. My nose is slightly crooked with one nostril smaller than the other, an asymmetry that has become more pronounced with age. I hate to disappoint you, but it doesn't make me look sinister! I'm neither beautiful nor ugly, old nor young. I'm unremarkable. That's my secret.

Whether I'm sipping a glass of crémant in the corner of a bar overlooking the Loire, or reading a book on the bus, people look through me or past me as if I am not there. They assume that because they don't see me, I don't notice them. But I miss nothing. All their secrets are woven into my tapestries. A long silken thread – where did it start? A woolly knot of rumour, a snippet of what someone said to someone else; heresy, perhaps, but who cares? Red, yellow or gold? Ochre for the sunflowers drooping just before harvest, and which red for the blood and which for the rose? Dip, dip, dip the wool into the dye.

Father Michael says more confessions have come out around our village looms than he ever heard in church. Don't scoff! All our stories are woven into this tapestry, hung high on the walls of our little church. Some secrets are deadly, best buried deep in the warp and the weft. But the truth is that none of us is what we seem.

I'm going to have to trust you. Can I do that? Swear it, now, before we begin! Good, good. Very good.

So, What's my name?

They call me Madame Mini after the mouse, because I'm small and don't talk very much. But that's because I see. Some say I'm a witch, but it's up to you what you believe. So, you think I'm an artisan? Don't insult me! Lighter, darker, a fraction. How best to tell the story? A margin for interpretation? Bien sûr! We tapestry makers, we're artists.

CHAPTER 1

It was done. Today she became a new person. Finally, she was free. Laura de Silva closed the door to her rented Lisbon apartment, kicked off her black patent Salvatore Ferragamo court shoes, raised her eyes to heaven, closed them, and heaved a huge sigh of relief. Miracles do happen. Suddenly, she was aware of her hands. They were trembling. Laura had come so far but it could all still go wrong. She had been in the city too long. It was time to disappear.

That morning, she had had her final meeting with her Portuguese lawyer. Of course, he knew or suspected, but in his line of work it was best not to pry. He had requested no more than the minimum information necessary to satisfy the regulations.

'Bloody Brussels and their red tape.' He had shrugged, an exaggerated gesture of despair.

But today the investments and property purchases had been concluded. Everything by the book, just as he had promised. She had paid him handsomely. That, she had learnt from her husband; everyone had a price. In return she had her prize, a shiny new Portuguese passport. She was a European citizen with a new name and a new life. French citizenship ought to have been hers by right, but without proper paperwork there was no proof. Screw them. She owed nothing to anyone. Money is power. That, too, she'd learnt from him. He couldn't get her now, could he?

She pulled herself together. No time to celebrate. Still so much to do.

In the bedroom, her mongrel thumped his tail in delight as if he sensed something was up, and Laura smiled. Her jaw ached. Was she still that tense?

She took a long last look at her old self in the mirror. She had grown up reflected in mirrors, moulded, trained, educated, forced into shape to serve the greater cause, to gratify others. A slim, elegant woman stared back at her. She appeared tall, but her height was deceptive; her apparent grace and poise were a feint, the product of practice and years of merciless training. Laura had reinvented herself many times over the course of her nearly sixty years. Today she was wearing a white designer shirt dress with black buttons and a neat contrasting velvet trim around the cuffs and collar, a large black hat, and sunglasses.

Laura removed the accessories then hesitated, deciding what to do with the dress. Might she need to play the rich, jet-setting lady in the future? No. The job was done. She would never go back. He would have to kill her first.

Tenderly, she folded the dress and stowed it in a black bin liner. Then she took a quick shower and dried herself. Wrapped in a large white towel, she stood in front of the bathroom mirror. The room was decorated in black marble and chrome, the mirror encircled by small light bulbs which reminded her of a tatty backstage dressing room from her younger life.

Her long black hair hung damp and loose about her shoulders. She made a feeble attempt to comb it out. But what was the point? Without hesitation, she picked up the scissors and dived in, snipping quickly and methodically at the tangle of curls. There was no regret, only a cautious welling of relief. Was this really happening? She had escaped. Freedom was there for the taking. Could it really be hers?

Gritting her teeth, she pulled viciously at her hair, which was shorter now, just above her shoulders. How she had hated her curls! They had marked her out since she was a child, branded her accursed.

A scent of lavender choked up inside her at the thought of her mother. One of Laura's earliest memoires was watering a few dusty pots of the scented flower on their rusty wrought-iron balcony. Mama used to say that lavender reminded her of happier times. The fragrance triggered a maelstrom of memories and emotions in Laura; the morning routine with her mother. Tight-lipped, thin, her face pinched with anxiety, Mama would brush roughly through her daughter's curls. Laura always knew there was something different that marked her out from other girls. She had blamed herself for being born that way. Tears would come to her eyes, she had learnt early never to protest at suffering or pain.

'Don't cry. Only babies cry. Her mother would pull Laura's hair harder, into neat, socialist pigtails. Tight, tighter, tighter, until Laura thought her scalp would be ripped off.

'Don't take it out on the child,' her father would admonish. How she had loved him! He had been the calm one, the one who would soothe them both with strokes and caresses, promising that everything would be alright – that was, until they broke him.

'What am I supposed to do?' Her mother would efficiently plait her daughter's pigtails, fastening them with patriotic red ribbons; the only flash of colour Laura remembered in her early world. 'If I cut the child's hair shorter it only curls more, and that's the trouble.'

Trouble: such a lazy word. People used it when the communal toilets got blocked, overflowing with backed-up faeces so that the whole building stank like a cesspit; or when there was a power cut; or when a new political campaign was on the wind; or when a neighbour failed to return home from work. Trouble: even before she could talk, little Laura new that it could be the code for terror. Terror came in many guises. She shivered at the thought of the Director, his crooked black teeth, the stink of garlic and tobacco on his breath, his wandering hands at costume fittings. He was like that with all the girls. They would giggle, shrug and roll their eyes.

'Better get used to it.'

Had she really been that young? She shuddered.

It had started innocently enough, with White Rabbit sweets, sitting on his knee as if he were some kind of prototype Communist Father Christmas. Gently, he would loosen a curl from its tight bun on the back of her head.

'So pretty,' he would coo, 'but curls are bourgeois. That makes you naughty. Are you a naughty girl?' And he would laugh and pinch her cheeks until they hurt. He had been the first. To be fair, he had waited until she was sixteen. They had given her birth control pills. Vitamins, they called them.

She hacked more viciously at her hair, as if pain could dissolve pain.

'Don't cry. Only babies cry!

In late spring heat, her rebellious hair was already starting to dry and curl. It was shorter on the left-hand side than the right, which produced a grim smile; she was a 'Rightist' after all! Calmer now, she trimmed gently, and not for the sake of vanity, she was way past that but because a lopsided hair-cut might attract attention. She ran her hand she through her short bob. She had stopped dyeing her hair only a month ago, but already the grey was showing at the roots.

Laying down the scissors, she stared defiantly at herself in the mirror.

'So there!' It had been her cascades of curls that had first attracted the man who had become her husband. He had forbidden her to cut them short, even as she aged. On their wedding night, he had released her hair gently, spreading it tenderly over her naked shoulders, stroking it, looping his index finger through individual curls. He had been so shy, so naïve. He had no idea that she had been raped as a child - for rape was what it had been, institutional, organised rape, and the teachers that were supposed to protect her had at worst facilitated and at best turned a blind eye. What else could they have done? Risk disgrace and imprisonment themselves?

Laura gathered up the collection of cosmetics, shampoos and soaps from the bathroom, then carried them into the bedroom and sorted them. She took only the essentials, contact lenses, spectacles, toothbrush, toothpaste, shower gel, and a cheap moisturiser she had bought from a supermarket. Her large armoury of Chanel, eyeshadows, foundation, serum, day cream, night cream, eyeliner, lipsticks, blemish corrector and powder was consigned to another bin liner. The rest was packed into a plastic bag at the bottom of a holdall. Changing her underwear, Laura slipped on a long emerald-green crinkle-cotton skirt and black T-shirt she had brought from Primark. She put on her 'no-show' socks, then strapped on a pair of expensive, well-padded white trainers. When it came to good shoes, she could not compromise.

The dog barked.

'Oui, oui. Soon, we are going.' Laura spoke to him in her French; it soothed her to do so. The dog had been with her barely a month, and it amazed her that he seemed to understand. She took the bin liners down to the cellar, leaving them with the recycling material in the hope that the beautiful dress at least might find a home. Returning via the stairs, not the lift, she put the dog on the lead, picked up her holdall, and locked the apartment door for the last time. Passing through the lobby when she knew the concierge would be on his break, she posted the keys in the letter box.

The heat was stifling in the underground garage. Quickly, she loaded the dog and holdall into a navy-blue van. When that was done, she looked over her shoulder to make sure the garage was deserted before opening one of the rear doors to peek inside and check the cargo. A large flat object, padded and wrapped in brown paper, sat slanted across the back of the van. It had been delivered from Rotterdam like that, and Laura had not dared attempt to move or open it, although the temptation to view and enjoy the treasure that she knew was in it had been great. Early that morning, before dawn, she had carefully padded the package with bedding, a roll-up camping mattress, pillows and towels. If the customs officers did stop her, it would look as if she were just moving house, which in a sense was true.

With a sigh of relief, Laura closed the rear door and climbed into the driving seat. With the sun behind them, she and the dog drove unnoticed out of Lisbon and took the E80 Autoestrada do Norte.

CHAPTER 2

France was bursting out of itself in the spring sunshine, and Laura was happy. Words jostled in her head, both in her own language and in French. Elation, joy, delight, ecstasy… how to describe it when, after a lifetime of waiting, suddenly you are free? The sunlight shimmered on the wide expanse of the river Loire, but it was late in the afternoon when Laura's van rolled across the single-track iron bridge from the south bank to the north. She had been on the road for two days, taking detours off the autoroutes through the villages, marvelling at the dilapidated manor houses and little châteaux with turrets or towers, churches and vineyards. She smiled at the giddy daffodils bobbing in the breeze along the verges, the trees in full blossom, pink, white, peach, rose, like great balls of candy floss. Laura's body was stiff and aching to the core, yet for once pain and discomfort did not trouble her. She was driving into a fairy tale, one of her own making; a dream, an illusion, constructed over a lifetime out of fragments in her mind: her mother's love, words of comfort whispered in French under the bedcovers to a little child, lullabies, prayers, hushed, buried deep, never told but never forgotten.

Dodo, l'enfant, dodo, the world is good. Sleep, child, sleep.

Who could have imagined that French would become the language of Laura's profession, the alien words that others struggled over but with which Laura feigned difficulty for fear of being unmasked? In later years, in better times, when they had access to books, Laura had fed her dream of France. She had taken language lessons in secret, devoured Balzac and Flaubert in translation, flirted with Racine, gorged on Pissarro, Cézanne, Renoir and Monet. She had always felt something inexplicable and wonderful about France within her, a feeling of peace and calm that had given her refuge at the worst of times. This gift, this imagining of another place, a land of art and culture, safety and love, was the only thing her mother had been able to bequeath her: a dream of beauty and peace, a shield against horror. And Laura had always kept it close, never shared it, least of all with her husband. 'Trust no one', her father had said, the night before her parents had sent her away. The mantra had served her well. It was the code by which she had lived her life. It was how she had survived.

Laura drove west for about three kilometres, then turned north at the crossroads in the market square of a village. The dog had fallen asleep some two hours ago and was snoring on the passenger seat. The spring light fell in slats through the woodland trees onto the road, making a fresh palette of undulating colours - green, bronze, yellow and gold – to give Laura the impression the sun was challenging her to a game of hide and seek.

Le Saut de Lion was a small village nestling between gently undulating hills. Geology had designed it to keep its secrets. At best the village appeared as a footnote in tourist guides; there might be a line or two of speculation about the obscure origins of the name and fanciful links to Richard the Lion Heart, and perhaps a reference to the two local vineyards and the fur-clad troglodytes who in prehistoric times had lived in caves in the hill. If, in the summer season, a few adventurous souls did turn off the châteaux route, they might say a quick prayer in the little church, paying a euro each to light a candle, have a light lunch of puffy bread pockets and pork pâté in the little bar in the square and visit Madame Mini's tapestry shop. The more sharp-eyed might spot the tiny plaque at the corner of the square, a list of five men, their names and ages:

Shot by the Nazis, March 1944.

Two of those killed had been just boys. The visitors might pause a second or two and shake their heads to mutter 'How sad', but they would soon be buying ice cream and taking selfies in front of the fountain in the village square. But for the unwary, the sensitive, who might be worn and weary of soul, the visit might be a risky affair. They might be enchanted by the whispers on the breeze, for Le Saut was an ancient and mysterious place. It drew people in on a whim and sometimes, it never let them go.

Laura drove up the gently sloping road into the village, past the post office and the pharmacy, then turned hard left down a narrow lane beside the primary school. At the bottom, she stopped at a large faded blue wooden gate. Painfully, she prised herself out of the driver's seat. Her muscles seized up too easily these days. Expertly she rolled her shoulders, her neck and her wrists then bent down to open the padlock hanging on its rusty iron chain. She pushed the gate open, got back into the van and reversed a little to ease the tight turn into the yard of her new home.

Sensing that the van had come to a stop, the dog lifted his head and gave a soft woof. Laura let him out of the van, then got his water bowl and filled it up. As he lapped up the water, she sipped the rest from the bottle and stared in wonder at the house, her house. She had visited only once before, a month ago, to view. It had been love at first sight. She had made a cash offer at twenty-five thousand euros below the asking price, which to her surprise had been accepted within the hour. When she had first escaped, she would have been content with just a few days of freedom; to wake up in the morning with no one watching, no expectation, no fear, no surveillance, threats or beatings. But in Lisbon the days had run into weeks, and there had been no sign of her husband or his henchman. She had relished each moment, each simple pleasure; a coffee and pastel de nata in the sunshine in a little square, followed by a cigarette and then another one with no one to stop her, no feelings of guilt or despair. Now here she was here, walking into her fairy tale.

The modest fifteenth-century farmhouse was built into the rock of the hill behind it. It had been abandoned at the end of the Second World War, only recently restored and largely modernised by the venders prior to sale. New PVC shutters in the light blue typical of the region had been fitted, and the living room and bedrooms had all been redone, as had the wiring and central heating, toilet and bathroom.

'Madame would have the great advantage of being able to install a new kitchen of her own design,' as the agent had said with a slick salesman's smile.

The large iron key was warm and heavy in Laura's hand. It had an intricate scroll top. She wondered how many hands it had passed through over the generations before it had got to her. It turned effortlessly in the freshly oiled lock. With the dog on the lead, Laura took a deep breath, pushed open the door and stepped over the stone threshold into her new home.

The front door opened directly into the large main sitting room. There she stood, reverently for a few seconds, sensing something beyond herself that she would have described simply, in her own language, as old. Inside, it was pitch-black, silent and still, and there was a musty smell overlaid with more than a hint of perhaps damp plaster and paint. Unlike at the time of her viewing, no one had taken the trouble to open the shutters, so Laura groped along the stone wall and turned on the lights. A series of tasteful modern spots had been installed to flatter the wide black beams, three of which ran crosswise across the room that spanned a good third of the front of the house. Laura set about opening the windows and throwing back the shutters. Having closed the front door, she let the dog off its lead. For once he did not run off but remained obediently at heel, looking at her quizzically. She bent down to pet him, snuggled into his neck and breathed in the comfort of his doggy smell. At length she stood up.

'Come on. Let's explore.'

The sitting room had been beautifully restored. What a contrast to the ultra-modern high-rise city from which Laura had first fled. She crossed to the new fireplace in the light local stone and caressed the large carved fleur de lys that was its centrepiece. It was smooth to the touch; it felt old, although it wasn't. Someone had left a bunch of dusty dried flowers in a glass on the mantelpiece. She did not mind. In a strange way, she found the tatty arrangement reassuring, for it meant that others had come before and she was not entirely alone.

Carefully, she tiptoed up the wooden staircase, not wanting to disturb the peace. The large front bedroom was directly above the sitting room. Once again she switched on the light and opened the windows and shutters. There were three tall double windows in this room. Feeling braver now, the dog sniffed at the foot of one of the original cupboards which were built deep into the old stone walls. Then, picking up more interesting scents, he pattered out of the room to explore.

Standing at the large central window, Laura fished a cigarette and yellow disposable lighter out of her shoulder bag. Lighting up, she inhaled and exhaled, watching the smoke float out of the window and disperse in the air.

Now at last she was ready to cry, letting the tears roll down her cheeks, catching some with her tongue, relishing the taste of salt as if it might heal her wounds.

'Mama, Baba, I'm here at the house. Maman, je suis arrivée. Can you hear me?'

The day was cooling quickly, the spring sunlight fading through yellow and peach to pink. Misty-eyed, Laura stared out over the garden. At the front of the house was a gravel driveway which led to an old open-fronted barn on the right. This was bounded by wide flower beds. A low stone wall with an old wrought-iron gate hung off its upper hinges between two tall stone gateposts, and this gateway led to a large garden that was walled on all three sides. Laura's land was fronted by a smallholding and another small hill, on top of which sat the main village and its ancient, narrow-spired church. Cosseted between the bigger and smaller hills, the house was hidden from the world. It lay quite literally at the foot of the church and that was how it had acquired its name. It had no house number, both name and address being simply *Au Pied de L'Eglise*: At the foot of the church.

Laura looked down into the garden itself, with its apple and plum trees in full bloom and some pink roses growing out of control in the borders. She did not heed the overgrown lawn, the tumbledown shed, the brambles and weeds; she smelt lavender and was a child again, snuggled up in bed, warming her feet on her mother's thighs. Her mother's cheek rested on her own, and she was whispering her daughter's favourite bedtime story.

Once upon a time in a far-off land there was a secret garden, and it all belonged to us, just you, me and Baba. Imagine, a little cottage in the garden which has high walls so no bad people could get in. Inside there is a pond with a fountain and a wooden bridge. There are apple trees and plum trees and beautiful flowers and butterflies. All day we play there, just the three of us. Baba climbs high into the branches of an old tree and hangs a swing from one of them. Together we sit on it, flying high into the sky with the birds, reaching for the clouds. We make a playhouse from old sheets over the garden chairs and catch fish from the pond. But do we eat the fish? No, for that would not be kind. We keep them in a bucket for a while and feed them breadcrumbs.

At this point, Mama would stretch out her arms as wide as she could under the bedcovers and then, quick as a flash, snap them shut around Laura. How they had laughed!

And at the end of the day, we are tired. We feast at a large wooden table under a red sun-shade; pork and chicken, and duck too, and cheese, and peaches and apricots and sweet rum cakes. And when we can eat no more, we sail away together to the land of dreams in a big wooden bed that is like a boat. Oh, ma petite, it is the most magical place. One day I will take you there.

Dodo, l'enfant, dodo, the world is good. Sleep, child, sleep.

In Le Saut the light was almost gone, and long shadows stalked Laura's garden. Suddenly her limbs flooded with a great heaviness. Pushing herself, she worked quickly to unload the van. She had travelled with only basic equipment plus a rice cooker. Food, crockery, cutlery and a corkscrew she had bought from Super U after picking up the keys from the estate agent in Saumur. Laura was used to extreme physical exertion and duress, but she had not anticipated such an overwhelming sense of fatigue. Panting, she struggled with the package in the back of the van; it was larger than she remembered. Cautiously, she manoeuvred it into the sitting room and stacked it carefully against the wall next to the fireplace.

The kitchen had not been updated for decades. A few empty cupboards still hung on the walls and there was a deep, old-fashioned sink with a rusty draining board. A new fridge had been delivered, as Laura had arranged; someone had kindly unpacked it and plugged it in, but left its packaging in the middle of the room. Laura did not care. She was ravenous. Washing her hands, she opened a bottle of red wine and took it to the sitting room. She had no energy for ceremony, so she drank from a mug and ate from packets. She devoured half a rotisserie chicken, feeding the dog as she went along. Biting tomatoes in half, she dipped them in salt and stuffed them between large chunks of a baguette. For dessert, she had bought a tarte à la crème topped with fresh raspberries, but when the time came, she was just too tired to tackle it. Eyes drooping, she locked up, put the perishables into the fridge and hauled herself upstairs by the wooden banister. In the empty bedroom she rolled out her sleeping mat and that of the dog, then positioned her pillow and sleeping bag. Sitting on the floor, she removed her shoes and briefly massaged her feet. Unwashed, fully dressed, with the dog at her side, she lay down. For the first time in years there was no torture, no lying awake for hours negotiating with pain. In an instant, she was fast asleep.

CHAPTER 3

Father Michael hung up his vestments on the yellow plastic hanger at the back of the vestry, locked away the communion wine and strolled across the square to the village's only café-bar. Just a handful of stalwarts ever turned up for the nine-thirty midweek Mass, but they came because they wanted to pray, and that was enough for him. People might scoff, but in the silence Father Michael could see the Holy Ghost descend among them. It came as a soft gold light at the moment of the Agnus Dei, and it made everything right. On this particular day, for once, the priest felt that all was well. The birds were singing, the sunshine warm on his face and, for a while at least, he was at peace with himself.

It had become a little ritual after midweek Mass for the priest and a few parishioners to adjourn to Henri and Céline Duguet's bar. As soon as Father Michael entered the establishment, conversation died. His pals from his former profession, his life before ordination, those that were still alive, called it 'deploying the dog collar'. It was like throwing an unexploded hand grenade into a crowded space. They used Father Michael to great effect on their twice-yearly reunions when they needed to clear themselves space at the bar or get a table at a busy restaurant. Today the dog collar had its usual effect.

'Bonjour, Father,' said the three workmen in steel-toed boots, their trousers padded at the knees, as they shuffled along like naughty schoolboys to make space for Father Michael. The men were covered in dust, their hands unwashed, and on a mid-morning break.

'Bonjour, Lucas. How's your father? We missed him at Madame Mini's last week.'

'It's his chest. The doctor has given him another course of antibiotics but the old soak is as bad-tempered as ever. Says he's not long for this world, but he's been saying that these last twenty years.' Lucas Santelli's appearance was indeed deceptive. Six feet tall and broad-shouldered as an ox, he had been blessed with curly blond hair and an angelic face. Now nearly sixty, he retained a full head of grey hair, and continued to benefit from the innocent charm of his looks in his business dealings.

Not long after Father Michael had first arrived in the parish, the elderly Madame Rossignol had described 'Young Santelli' as a thug and a cheat. 'Always has been, ever since he was a boy. Like his father before him, and the good Lord forgive me, if one day I don't put an end to all this.'

But Father Michael always took what was said in the shadows of the village confessional box with a generous pinch of salt. Feuds that had begun generations ago in the region had festered over the years to the point when no one could, or would, remember why they had started in the first place. In the commune, forgiveness, it seemed, was often in short supply.

But despite himself, Father Michael had eventually come to agree with Madame Rossignol's assessment. The man was a bully. God alone knew, he had come across enough of them, lived with them, trained them. It didn't matter what forsaken sink-hole they had emerged from and some of them were indeed slippery bastards born with silver spoons in their mouths. They were all little men who attempted to disguise their own inadequacies with bluff, bravado and brutality to those weaker than themselves. Young Santelli was a vocal member of the Rassamblement National and had been involved in assorted blockades, rallies and assorted punch-ups over the years. Whenever there was trouble, Young Santelli and his associates were more than likely to be involved. On occasions, Father Michael had been tempted to land a couple of punches on Lucas Santelli's nose and teach the man a lesson himself. But he doubted the Church would have approved.

'Votre George.' The patron, Henri Duguet, unshaven, a damp tea-towel thrown over his shoulder, plonked down Father Michael's espresso in front of him and fished two bags of sugar from the basket behind the bar.

The 'votre George' was a reference to the actor George Clooney, and this was something of a local joke. A couple of years' ago, Duguet's glamorous younger second wife, Céline, had decided that the time had come for some changes; the dingy, smoke-filled, misogynistic watering hole that passed as a café had to be dragged into the twenty-first century. If the bar were to balance its books, it needed to attract women and summer tourists. A little revolution; that, she decided, was what was needed.

Céline had drawn up a business plan and commissioned an interior designer from Tours. The wobbly pre-war wooden tables and beer-stained wooden floor were replaced with a gleaming white marble-topped bar along with red leather bar stools. There were cream-coloured floor tiles, new metal tables and matching chairs. There were even two American-style seating booths and mirrors, one on each side of the bar. Folding floor-to-ceiling windows were also installed so that in the spring and summer the whole of the café could be opened to the square. In the summer, Henri and Céline would set up tables outside, each decked with a jaunty red and white checked tablecloth, a pot of fresh basil, and shaded with large white sunshades.

Their investment soon paid off. In season, the tourists came. Duguet, too, would smarten himself up. He got a haircut and shaved every day. Instead of slouching about in a pair of jeans and grubby sweat-shirt, he would wear crisply ironed navy shorts, a turquoise polo shirt and matching suede deck shoes. The grumpy old bastard had transformed himself into a handsome, suave café owner who charmed the tourists, especially the English and Dutch ladies.

'Heaven knows what they see in him!' But all the changes, Céline insisted, were required in the tourist business. Her revolution also greatly improved the antiquated sanitation of the café. No longer were the ladies obliged to walk past the men at the two urinals in the back corridor and then across a couple of duckboards to a wooden shed in the yard outside. Miraculously in what was officially a UNESCO World Heritage area, planning permission had been obtained for a discreet rear brick extension with Velux windows. It contained separate facilities for each sex, with a cubicle adapted to accommodate wheelchair access and a changing table for babies. It even had large bottle-green glass washbasins mounted on a marble counter, and automatic taps. When, in the middle of their first high season, some visitors from Paris had suggested to the tight-fisted Duguet that segregated toilet facilities were discriminatory and that such modernisation had in fact been a retrograde step, the patron had threatened to bounce the complainant on his backside, one cobble at a time, down the street.

But the highlight of the refit as far as the locals were concerned was the acquisition of a shiny, new, bright-red coffee machine. Above it, Céline hung a picture of George Clooney seductively sipping his Nespresso. Thereafter, the villagers acquired the habit of asking for 'un George' whenever they wanted a strong black coffee. Prices increased, of course, which engendered hours of moaning about the loss of purchasing power and a general lamentation about the decline in traditional French values. But in the end it was grudgingly admitted that the new-fangled Italian machine did produce a beverage superior to the slurry Duguet had previously passed off as coffee.

Father Michael tore the top off one of the sugar packets, tipped the entire contents and stirred his coffee carefully, before picking it up and going over to join three of his female parishioners who were seated at a table to the right at the front of the bar.

The folding doors were open, and the ladies were cautiously dangling their feet in the sunshine. They had bought croissants from the bakery and were eating them out of paper bags. One of the ladies, who amply filled her chair, moved both it and her coffee cup to create some space for the priest to join them. She was known as La Folle Anglaise and was sitting next to the elderly Madame Rossignol, who was also drinking coffee, and Madame Mini, who occupied her regular corner perch and nursed her customary morning glass of Crémant. La Folle Anglaise, whose real name was Madeleine Brown, was an English woman who had married a Frenchman thirty years ago and moved to the village from Paris after her husband had been tragically killed in a car accident. A former French teacher in England, she spoke and wrote excellent French. Grammatically, she was far more accurate than many native speakers but she still retained a detectable English accent. This, combined with her weight, size and tendency to bulldoze through all opposition to her latest initiatives in the commune, was the reason for nickname; the Mad English woman. After over twenty years in the village, she was just about accepted and had risen to be Secretary of the Commune's administrative committee. She took everything in good part, even signing administrative e-mails about variations to rubbish bin collection times and temporary contraflow systems with an affectionate, 'Maddy, La Folle Anglaise.'

Maddy never took no for an answer and as far as Father Michael was aware, she had no enemies. She was a Protestant, of course, Church of England. She was very precise about that, but Father Michael was a not a conventional French curé, and if she presented herself at the communion rail, he wasn't going to turn her away. She was also a talented artist, and it was La Folle Anglaise who had been the main mover and shaker behind the commune's tapestry initiative.

And so Father Michael sat in companionable silence with her and her companions: Madame Rossignol, who looked about seventy-five but was in fact coming up for ninety-three, was someone you didn't want to mess with; and Madame Mini, the enigmatic Tapestry teacher, was armed as ever with her magic wand, a bright pink walking stick decorated with silver stars. Watching the three women, Father Michael decided that if the men of the village thought they were in charge, they were kidding themselves.

'Have you heard about Old Blanchard's pile of old stones? The deal went through last week. Apparently, the new owner has already moved in,' one of Santelli's younger companions said from the back of the bar.

'Bloody miracle, that. How long has the place been empty?'

No one answered.

'Seems to be cursed that house. Got bad blood.' said Santelli's companion, unaware of the pot he was stirring.

'Well, he's welcome to it, whoever he is,' Young Santelli boomed so loudly that everyone could hear. 'They should have razed that place to the ground years ago. Refused to work on it, I did. Wasn't going in to touch the place with a barge-pole. None of the boys from around here would, either. In the end, the family had to bring their own contractors in from down south. Work still not finished, or so they say.'

'Apparently she's a foreigner, Japanese or something.' The youngest of Santelli's companions was enjoying being the source of new information.

'I heard she was Portuguese.'

'Portuguese, Nip, same difference, bloody foreigners. Don't want any more of that sort round here. Send them all back to where they come from. France is for the French.' Normally no one would have paid any attention to Santelli. Privately, that's what many in the region thought. But not everyone. Not that day.

Up rose the tall, slim figure of Madame Rossignol from her

chair. Drawing her purse from her handbag as if to arm herself, she walked purposefully up to the bar and confronted Santelli.

'And just what are you going to do for work if all the foreigners in the region leave? Who else is going to invest in our old piles of stones, if not the English and other foreigners?' She tapped Young Santelli three times on his chest with her bony index finger. 'And who are you to talk? Your grandfather was an Italian, if my memory serves me correctly.'

The old lady placed some euros on the counter and turned to walk out of the bar.

'Go back to where you came from with all the other bloody foreigners, why don't you? Good riddance to bad rubbish! Keep the change, Henri, mon ami. Come on, ladies!'

CHAPTER 4

It was pitch-black when Laura woke with a start. Where was she? Where was he? Her body was tense and alert, primed by habit for onslaught, anticipating the soft cruel barrage that had been his morning routine. He would start gently with a caress of her neck. For years she had almost believed he was trying to be kind, to make up for the day before, the month before, and the year before that. Perhaps it had all never happened? Had she taken it the wrong way, and she was the one at fault? She should try harder to please him, to be a good wife.

'Get up, lazy bones.' He would tweak the nipple of her right breast, which he called her tit. He insisted that she slept naked, even in the winter when she complained of cold. He would go at her a second time, pinching and twisting the nipple hard, and if she pushed away his hand, his sneering response was always the same, a short sharp slap on the cheek, hard enough to hurt, but not forceful enough to leave a mark or a bruise.

'Can't you take a joke? No sense of humour, wife, that's your trouble.'

Laura heard the patter of the dog's paws on the tiled floor downstairs. A fuzzy reality dawned. She was in France, at home. Relief flooded from head to toe like a shower of warm summer rain. She relaxed back onto the pillow and stretched.

Then, in the darkness, something strange happened:- she felt herself smile. Could it be? Could it really be? She wriggled her toes, testing the sense of easy delight, then rolled over on her camping mattress and buried her head in the pillow. Just another hour.

It was the dog who eventually woke her, nuzzling her face with his wet nose. She pulled him to her and stroked his neck.

She got up quickly. That was her mistake. A shot of pain raked through her feet, ankles and knees, and grated in her hips, its violence snatching her breath away.

'Oh God!' How could she have been so stupid? How could she have believed, even for one second, that in escaping him she might be free of pain? She sniffed, tears of frustration, betrayal and disappointment behind her eyes. She had tried so hard, always done her best, and when the Party had asked for more she had strained every sinew to give more than her best. What had she done to deserve this? Would she ever be free of this torture, even for a day? It was not just the physical pain, but the crushing sense of loneliness and despair it engendered.

'Don't cry! Only babies cry.' she admonished herself in her mother tongue. She was good at hiding her emotions. Was she even capable of being honest anymore? She had lied and cheated to get to France; a small fraud and then a bigger one and a bigger one still, until at last she had seen a way out: a new name, a new passport, a new life. In her life, truth had always been defined by others, and once upon a time she would have died for it. But the truth to which she had dedicated her young life had been a false idol. The only faith she believed in now was the one her mother had bequeathed her, the beautiful dream of a safe place in a far-away country called France.

Laura hobbled over to the central window and unhitched the shutters, right first then left, deliberately, an old and puerile form of rebellion which still gave her a peculiar sense of satisfaction. Birdsong and sunlight rushed in and she gasped again, this time with joy. Ratcheting her spine to vertical, she walked slowly back to the middle of the room. Gingerly, she sat down in the slice of sunlight, raising her face, relishing the spring warmth. What time was it? The sun was high in the sky. Was it already noon? With a sigh she resigned herself to her morning warm-up routine, without which she was a virtual cripple.

She began by massaging each toe, coaxing warmth and movement into the balls of her feet. Her toes were so ugly and deformed that it distressed her to look at them, although she knew every joint, muscle and sinew, every pressure point. She worked up to her ankles, circling them right then left, flexing and re-flexing before committing herself to a long, slow forward bend. Breathe, breathe, breathe, release and down again, until her cheek rested on her knees. She would not be beaten by it, not now when she had come so far. She then lay on her back on the hard floor; she was no stranger to that. She stretched up to lengthen her spine, took a deep breath, and pulled one thigh to her and then the other, prompting another surge of pain. Breathe, breathe, breathe. Wait, that's right, work through it. The hips were where the damage was worst. Back then, no one cared about the long-term cost to their health. There had been no physiotherapists, no modern knowledge or expertise. They had simply been children whose bodies and minds were to be moulded to serve the cause without regard to the personal cost.

Laura washed, dressed and descended to the kitchen. For breakfast she took the tarte from the previous evening and a banana. She ate quickly, furtively, like a naughty child expecting a slap at any time, and washed the food down with couple of anti-inflammatories and a cup of tea. Then, taking a torch, she unlocked the door at the back of the kitchen and took the steps down to the cellar.

A lone light bulb covered in cobwebs dimly lit a room that had been given rudimentary breeze-block walls. The cellars had been carved under the road and into the rock. They were, as the estate agent had whispered with some trepidation, very old, and in the Middle Ages they had been used to farm mushrooms. Laura flashed the torch. To the left and right were crudely carved stone archways. She took the left-hand one. It led to a passage about six feet wide which ran along the back of the house. After about ten metres it descended right by four uneven steps and opened to a huge empty cave.

Laura shivered in the chill air. The silence was so thick it seemed to suck in the light from her torch. She switched off the beam and stood in the blackness. Others had been here before, and she was just the latest pilgrim. She imagined snow outside, prowling lions and tigers, cavemen huddled around an open fire. Suddenly, for a second, she thought she heard gruff young men's voices, someone shouting orders and then singing. They rushed past like a blast of air, like opening the window of a moving car and quickly closing it again. Startled, Laura cast the torch beam over the rock. There was no sign of another passage, a light or a door. An alternative way out would have been impossible, she rationalised, because the cave was already deep in the hill with no other dwellings nearby.

And yet she was not afraid. If asked, she would have said most firmly that she did not believe in religious superstition, ghosts or spirits; that was what the Party had taught her. She would not tell anyone that she lived with them all the time, ghosts from the past, memories, some might call them. Standing in the silence, Laura was overcome with a heavy calm, a sense that her being here in this place was meant to be.

Returning to the breeze-blocked room, she peered down four uneven stone steps through the right-hand arch. It led to a much narrower passage, the roof descending to a height of about three feet at the back. It occurred to Laura, not for the first time, that she could hide the painting in the cellar. She could block up the door from the kitchen and no one would ever find it.

Laura was moving more easily now, but after the unaccustomed long drive of the last few days, she was bone-tired. How else could she explain the strange voices? She found an old deck-chair in the laundry, its red, white and blue stripes sun-bleached to a mélange of muddy browns. Dusting it down, she carried it out into the garden and placed it under a cherry tree. Then she did something she had never done in her life; she sat in the full glare of the sun, the pink blossom floating down like confetti around her, dotting the uneven lawn. Who was there to stop her? And so what if she freckled her nose and got a tan? After a while, she closed her eyes, letting the soft breeze caress her face, soaking up the gentle spring warmth. Bliss!

For the last twenty years she had lived in a city penthouse apartment on the thirty-seventh floor, air-conditioned when her husband would allow it. For as long as she could remember, her life had been restricted, managed and controlled. In more recent years, a driver had taken her from gym and studio to designer shops, hotels and malls. In the evenings there would be appearances and functions, an international tennis competition, a film premiere, a dinner with investors, the launch of an art exhibition. 'Businessman and well-known patron of the arts and his wife', that's how the glossy magazines described them. But it was a front, designed to show how educated, respectable and cosmopolitan he was. Laura, with her impeccable manners and passable English, was simply part of his act. People envied her success, her graceful figure and affluent lifestyle. Hadn't she done well for herself? Wasn't she lucky!

But the truth was that she had been living in hell, a luxurious, hermetically sealed glass and marble hell with never the chirping of birds nor a breath of fresh air to welcome the day.

Here in France, Laura could fill her lungs and breathe the spring air. The latter had a chilly back note, but the sun was warming the earth and the scents were rising. There was the smell of soil and the promise of a harvest yet to come. Laura's skin tingled with pleasure. There was no longer anything she wanted to change. Nothing could be better than this moment, right here, in her own garden in France with the dog resting at her feet. Sighing, she abandoned herself to the warmth, letting it seep into her aching muscles and bones. Everything seemed to be a kaleidoscope of colours, sensations and textures. Surrendering to her inner world, she watched them swirl and metamorphose, tight black spots of acute pain softening into red and then pink and dissolving into yellow and gold until they collapsed to nothing.

Laura awoke to the sound of the dog barking. Teeth bared, wolf-like, he was engaged in a stand-off with a scrawny black cat. The cat, clearly surprised to find a dog occupying what had hitherto been its uncontested territory, was standing its ground. Back arched, it hissed and spat. The dog circled, growling, driving back the cat inch by inch into a corner. Wait, wait, wait. The moment came. With a roar, the dog sprang forward. A horrendous roaring, screeching, spitting, whirling melee ensued. Laura jumped up, frantically calling off the dog, but he took no notice. He had the cat by the tail. But the feline was quicker, more agile. Spinning round, it raked the dog's face with its claws, causing him to let go. Then it ran, scrabbling up the ivy on the back garden wall and escaped to the other side, leaving the dog barking furiously beneath.

It took Laura a while to clean up the animal. He was bleeding, but the wounds were superficial. Nevertheless, she was shaken. She had never seen the dog behave like that before. She was no stranger to violence, the naked, feral, primeval kind where neighbours beat friends in the street. Civilisation was superficial; she had seen it fall apart. On this occasion, she chose to blame herself. She had been so tired and she had neglected the dog. The poor creature had been cooped up in the van for days. He needed exercise. Tomorrow, she would take him for a long walk. For now, she found a large stick, and they began to play.

It was late afternoon before the dog grew tired and retreated into the house. The church bells began to ring, a deep resonant gong that echoed off the hills and across the village. When silence came, Laura turned towards the house. A few swallows had returned and swooped over her roof-top, catching insects. Was it she who had brought the birds with her on her long journey from the south, or the birds that had brought her? She watched them fly in and out of the nooks in the escarpment behind the house. They were building their nests, just like she was intending to do. But how long could this freedom, this liberation, last? Liberation! What a fine word. It had such dignity. She chewed it over in her mouth, pouting her lips, rehearsing the sound in French.

Had he found out yet? Had he realised what she'd done, what she'd actually done? Was he missing her? Probably not. First things first. He would have checked the jewels, the diamond, ruby and emerald rings, necklaces and earrings, the expensive trophies he had bought her over the years. How she would have loved to have been there, to have seen his face, for she had not taken a thing! No doubt he would be consoling himself with his latest mistress, an Olympic gymnast. Young, nubile, tough, calculating. Good luck to her, for he was a monster, a Jekyll and Hyde. But one thing was certain. One day, maybe tomorrow, maybe next week, or in a year or ten years, he would come for Laura. He would consider her desertion a humiliation, a loss of face. A man like that never admitted defeat; he would have to have the last word, and when he did, God help her. Laura had no family and no connections. All her friends were his friends. He had made sure of that.

She imagined his rage on discovering that she was gone, not just lost or delayed or delinquent, his words again, not hers. Returning home alone, he would curse his secretary, then shout for the maid, ordering her to make his favourite chicken wings. The poor woman, knowing what was coming in a few seconds, would scuttle back to the kitchen, her plastic slippers flapping double time. He would dock his phone and play a singer he had first heard in his headphones on an international trip's in-flight playlist. He told Laura that she had a voice like an angel. Eyes narrowed to slits, he would eat the whole plate of chicken wings, sucking on the skin, spitting the bones onto the table. How many times had he made Laura sit and watch him do it? To torment her, he would throw her one wing as if she were a dog, and order her to eat. Eyes down, she would do as she was told. It was easier that way. And when he was done, he would wipe his mouth with his cotton napkin and pick at his teeth with the stainless toothpick which he carried in its silver case in his shirt pocket. He was, he would declare, in the process of deciding sentence. Such retrograde and irresponsible behaviour on her part needed punishment. What pompous words, but the mere thought of them made Laura's shoulder muscles tighten in anticipation of what she knew was to come. He was a clever, ruthless charmer, someone who had clawed his way up, making the right connections, playing the game. She had no illusions about the potency of naked money mixed with unfettered political power or the extent of his international networks.

And when he discovered what she had done, when he found her, what would his sentence be then?

Her mind was fully alert now, calculating quickly, back in survival mode. Who knew her story, all of it? Of course, the artist himself, but he had been grateful for the money and emigrated to Canada with his wife and daughter. He would not easily betray her; he had too much to lose. Laura had been very careful to cover her tracks. No one knew the full story except herself. That part had been easy, for there was now no one left to confide in, no one left she needed to protect, no one who cared.

In the end, it had all been so simple. He had meetings in Hong Kong. As always, she'd accompanied him. She was going to meet their regular art dealer. Wisely, she had judged it best to keep up appearances even as her plan reached its end point. But this time, things were different. Not only was everything ready, but Laura's driver had taken unexpected leave to return to his home village because his mother was dying. Her husband was generous with staff, especially the thick-fisted, vindictive gorilla of a man whom he employed to mind her. The gorilla and her husband went way back, well before Laura's time. That was how he was able to manage people. It was the way his system worked. He would pay generously, do favours, pull a string or two here and there for a daughter or son, a mother, or a friend of a friend. Before long, a person's whole family depended on his network and goodwill.

'Such a good man, a good man,' people said, nodding their heads approvingly. But when the time came to call in a favour or a debt, he was merciless.

But did her husband really think that after all the years of cruelty he had broken her, that she had given up, that she would continue to lie down and take it? She had come close at times, taking the kitchen chopper while he was sleeping. One slash across his throat, that's all it would have taken. But it would have finished with a trial, a death sentence, a bullet in her brain. She was not going to afford him the final victory.

Bizarrely, when it came to it, that final morning in Hong Kong, she had just strolled through the chaos into an Indian travel agent and bought a ticket on the midday-flight to Manila. Once there, she had picked up a forged Filipino passport in a new name. It was only ever meant to get her to

Europe, and then she would get rid of it. From Manila, she had boarded the late evening flight to Los Angeles, then taken the Greyhound bus to New York. If he did manage to pick up her trail, she hoped he would focus his search there. She had been meticulous in laying the ground. It had all been years in the planning. On their many previous trips to the city, she had enthused about the art galleries, the restaurants and the fashion houses. She would smile, pat his arm and be good. She would play the coquette.

'I just love NYC.'

But Laura had not stayed long in the Big Apple. She got a cancellation on the *QEII* to London, then travelled on the Eurostar to Paris, from where she took another train to Lisbon. And the most amazing thing of all, the painting? Of all the valuable art that had passed through her hands, it had been the only one ever to have truly touched her heart, so much so that she had been unable to part with it. Miraculously, it had arrived just one-week later by sea, just as she had prearranged. Unbelievable! Easy, too easy, perhaps?

The dog barked from the kitchen door. The cat had returned, and now paraded defiantly along the length of the wall. Laura's stomach started to rumble but she was reluctant to leave the glory of the day. She decided to put on a coat and take a picnic into the garden. The sky dissolved into a rose peach behind the church spire. Laura opened a bottle of wine and broke pieces of baguette, which she ate with cheese and olives. The trees rustled in the breeze, shadows emerged, and she felt the spirits of her parents close by. Her father sat cross-legged at her side, smoking a cigarette, the scent of it soothing her like sandalwood in a temple. Her mother, at the far end of the rug, was cutting the boudin sausage with her dainty, frost-chapped hands. In that moment Laura could almost reach out and touch them as if they were sharing her food, and yet she could not see their faces. She could never see their faces. The truth was, she had forgotten what they looked like, and any photographs there might have been had long since been lost. But, then, it seemed to Laura that she had been in this place in a past life and had come home.

She lifted her eyes to the fast-darkening sky. So what if he did find her? This day of homecoming had been hers. This moment was hers, and he could not take that from her. As for the painting, why should she hide it in the darkness, giving it up to mould and decay? Beautiful things were made to be enjoyed. She would hang it on the sitting room wall for all to see, and to hell with the consequences.

CHAPTER 5

Bill Winston ought to have heeded his wife's warnings and not been so reckless with his family's good fortune, but he was a stubborn man. That Wednesday in his ice cream store had just been a regular day. The thaw had come, and they had only recently re-opened after their annual winter closure. Business was picking up, and a rainbow of tourist faces passed in front of the ice cream counter. They came from all over the world to gasp and gawp at the magnificence that was the Canadian Rockies but by the time they had driven up the Icefield Parkway and pottered about on the Athabasca Glacier and the Skywalk, they had had enough of wilderness and were ready for an ice cream. Bill and his wife, Vivien, were ready to oblige. Their store was in the middle of Jasper, right on the tourist trail. Mountains of glistening colours, a myriad of flavours; dark chocolate, mint, choc chip, raspberry, almond milk, pistachio, cookie dough, blue bubble-gum, pink bubble-gum, lemon soufflé, coconut, rocky road: 'Which one's yours?'

Bill would never hurry a customer to choose. 'Take all the time in the world, sir. Sure, come back tomorrow! Have a nice day!'

He loved to watch the children's faces, black, white, brown, sun-kissed all, as they chose their ice creams. The ohs and ahs, the shy smiles and giggles, the sparkling excitement in their eyes, whispered consultations and negotiations with parents in languages he did not always understand. But my! How their eyes would dance when he presented them with their prizes! For the nice kids, the particularly polite, considerate and well-behaved, those who taught him a little of their own language, there would be a bonus; an extra-big scoop, a little on the side. 'One scoop, two scoops, three scoops, Mega Cup Special deal?'

It was a habit that earned him daily admonishment from his sharp-tongued wife, especially during the height of the summer months. Did he think that money fell down from heaven? They weren't running a charity. There were his daughter's school fees to pay.

But Bill couldn't help himself; he loved the children who came to his shop, even those who were spoilt and over-indulged. If it had been up to him, he would have given them all their ice creams for free. There had never been treats when he was a child. One particularly harsh winter, his family had nearly starved. It was only the rabbits they kept and bred in a hutch that had made the difference between life and death. For a reason he had never understood, his father had given him the job of wringing the poor creatures' necks. Tighter and tighter he would squeeze. Their oxygen-starved eyes and the crack of the bone as it broke were the stuff of his nightmares.

Never in his wildest dreams could Bill Winston have imagined that he and his wife would become the proud proprietors of a money-spinning ice cream store in Canada. They had been teachers back in their home country. And even if they had dreamed of a new life in the beautiful land that was the USA or the no less beautiful Canada, he never could have predicted the way it would come about. Did he feel bad about it? Hell no! On the contrary; it had given him immense satisfaction to pull the wool over the eyes of the artistic élite at the Academy of Arts. He had come from the wrong social class for the time and had never been accepted, never had a chance. It was ironic that the one thing he had learnt at the Academy was how to copy, to imitate, meticulously. The hierarchical teaching methods had squeezed the creativity out of him. 'Think you're something special, son? You know nothing. Copy the master and then we'll see' Sometimes when sitting on his deck late on a Canadian summer's night, Bill Winston would raise a can of beer to them and chuckle. Self-righteous fools, the whole damn lot of them!

He'd never told his wife the full story of how he had met the beautiful young woman with the curly hair on the Shanghai Waterfront in the spring of 1986, but the encounter was etched on the front of his mind. The political winds were changing, and for some reason girls had judged it safe to start wearing pretty, feminine things. They popped up like spring flowers after decades of winter, and the young Bill had been entranced. Never before had he seen real women, women like those hitherto confined to foreign advertisements, wearing lipstick, high heels and flowery dresses with delicate lace collars. In his own way, the young Bill was also testing the waters as a painter, cautiously displaying a few small Monet-style oils of the old colonial waterfront and doing charcoal portraits for sale. Once, an Englishman had told him that the Waterfront was modelled on that in Liverpool. He was amazed. They hadn't taught that at school.

Then one day she had just glided into his life, strolled out of the sunshine on the arm of a tall dandy of a chap. Bill had disliked him immediately. He was a huge man, well over six feet tall, the first of a new brash breed, strutting about in sunglasses, leather jacket and jeans. She, on the other hand, was wearing a large white sun-hat and a simple home-made purple and white spotted dress that fluttered enticingly around her long legs. In an instant she had captivated him with her grace and style.

'Oh, look! Aren't these delightful?' Pulling her skirt around her for modesty, she had squatted down to view Bill's paintings, which he had displayed along the river wall. She removed her sunglasses and peeped up at him from under the brim of her hat, looking at him with in that gentle way of hers, which made the person she was addressing feel as if they were the most important in the world. In that instant, Bill knew she was a sensitive soul, a fellow traveller. When her boyfriend had paid him a few pennies to sketch, Bill's heart had leapt for joy.

Afterwards she had taken his business card, and over the years one thing had led to another; small purchases and commissions for her apartment. She liked the French Impressionists, and he was good at copying their work. The truth was that neither of them had set out to do what they had ended up doing together. As the years had passed and her circumstances changed, they had just fallen into it. Eventually he was moonlighting full-time for her, working on big commissions in his tiny flat. He loved the challenge of copying a masterwork and was obsessive about brushstroke, paint and detail. He left the forging of the artist's signature to the end, but every time he came to put his brush to canvas, he was sick with fear and would smoke half a packet of cigarettes before attempting the final deed.

His wife had never actually asked him directly about money, but when it started rolling in, she put two and two together and made four. Didn't everyone make fakes in those days, fake Gucci handbags, fake Prada, fake Louis Vuitton, fake Rolex, fake Reeboks? Who cared? What were a few silly paintings? It was Vivien, a maths teacher and ever the pragmatist, who had suggested their move to Canada to him, the dreamer of the pair. Bless her!

They had purchased the ice cream business not long after arriving there. Over dim sum with friends in Vancouver, she had heard that the business was for sale as a going concern. They had both always worked, and she wanted Bill to give up painting; with a chequered past like his, it was becoming too risky. One spring day, just after the snows had melted, they had made the long drive from Vancouver to Jasper. Bill had been astounded by the vastness of the wilderness, and it struck him forcefully that here in Canada there would no longer be any constraints, no one to mark him right or wrong. He couldn't wait to get to the easel and create visions of his own. In Jasper, Vivien had gone over their finances and the accounts of the ice cream business in great detail and had succeeded in negotiating and concluding a purchase at significantly below the asking price.

The subsequent years had passed in a steady routine. Bill and Vivien ran the shop during the spring and summer months and into the early fall. Just before the nights started to really draw in, they would shut up the shop and Vivien would return to their house in a suburb of Vancouver. As for Bill Winston, not his real name, of course, he would load his pick-up truck and head up to a cabin outside Jasper to paint. Vivien had reluctantly agreed to compromise on Bill's art after their only daughter had graduated high school and gone to university. Her key condition was that Bill should not exhibit or sell any of his paintings, lest it drew attention to himself and the family. They had argued at length about it.

Who would recognise this man now? He'd chosen 'Bill', after Bill Clinton and 'Winston' after Churchill, two strong leaders he greatly admired – and neither name bore any relation to his own. Besides, he'd gone native and plump on a North American diet; some days he barely recognised his swollen pork-pie self. At first, Vivien had had her way, anything for a quiet life. But what was the point of painting if one could not display one's work? Last year the temptation had been too great, and Bill had secretly placed half a dozen or so canvases with a gallery in Whistler. They had sold quickly and easily, and he had won a prize for new talent, the first public accolade of his life. He thought it hilarious for a man in his sixties and about the oldest, murkiest talent on the block. He had not dared tell Vivien about the paintings or the sale. What she didn't know, he judged, wouldn't hurt her.

The last customers in the shop that evening were a grumpy French couple. When he had first arrived in Canada, Bill had struggled to tell white people apart from each other. He thought they all looked the same. But this man was different. The shape of his head for some amusing reason reminded Bill of a peanut, and he had protruding cheek-bones and a prominent nose. With copious gesticulation, the man complained to Bill that he had thought Canada was a bilingual country and that he would be able to speak French throughout his travels. 'But it's not true!' The man rolled his eyes. 'I have to speak English and it's painful for me.'

Bill was tired and irritated. Efficiently, he served the man his tiramisu ice cream and was relieved to shut up shop as soon as the couple left.

The Winston's' Jasper home was on the outskirts of town, backing onto the forest. Putting on his slippers, Bill took a beer from the fridge and went out onto the deck. Sipping his beer, ears pricked, he interrogated the shadows among the trees, anticipating softly shifting tones of darkness that might betray the presence of a bear. After a while he lit a cigarette and idly scrolled through the newsfeed from his home country on his phone.

'Prominent socialite and art collector disappears. Suspicion of tax evasion'.

Bile rose at the back of Bill Winston's mouth. 'Disappeared' or 'been disappeared'? The distinction was vital. He read on. There was a picture of the woman he had first met on the Waterfront all those years ago at the launch of a new contemporary art exhibition in Hong Kong. She had aged since their last meeting, but the curly hair that he had sketched and had fantasised about was still jet-black and cascaded down her bare right shoulder.

A distant rustle told him that a black bear was foraging on the edge of the forest. Bill spat the bile from his mouth. Briefly he thought of sending the woman an email to ask if all was well. There had been no contact since the final blockbuster commission had been completed and he had emigrated to Canada; nonetheless, he still had the email address of her company based in the Cayman Islands. Bill dismissed the idea almost as soon as he thought of it. His wife had been right to be anxious. They were watching, always watching. He shivered. He knew now that he had been naïve to think that just because they lived a world away, he could escape his past.

In the shadows, the bear turned and walked unhurriedly away, its great bulk merging into the undergrowth. One way or another, Bill Winston knew the hunt was on.

CHAPTER 6

For years Laura had survived day to day, never knowing where the next blow or verbal assault might land, keeping herself going by planning her escape, turning every opportunity to her advantage. Beyond securing independent finance, which was the foundation of everything, she had thought little about what she would do with her liberty, for it had seemed an impossible dream. Striving towards it had been a purpose in itself, giving her a reason to carry on. Physical pain, she could cope with. She had lived with it as long as she could remember but never had she anticipated that once free, she might be swallowed up by exhaustion. She knew she had burned her bridges and there could be no going back, but coming to terms with the reality of exile and the fact she had given up her people and her homeland was a different matter. She was alone in a foreign land with no one to help her, where no one cared. Laura would snooze for hours in the spring sunshine, even the smallest task leaving her drained. At times the great drowning lethargy had threatened to engulf her completely.

It was the garden centre that saved her, giving her fresh purpose during her first month in France. She came across it quite by accident on a supermarket run. The display of garden fountains and hundreds of stone statues and sculptures outside had beguiled her and drawn her in: a Roman goddess, an owl, a pair of huge embracing hands, a child reading a book, a naked curly-haired Greek man, a winged griffin, a small army of terracotta warriors next to the soft forms of a man and woman in an embrace. There had been no such things as garden centres in her own country, not on such a scale at least, for she came from an urban world where the majority lived in apartments. The most people aspired to would be a few vegetables and flowers on a balcony or rooftop, and small water features were in vogue in some sitting rooms and hallways.

It was early one midweek morning when Laura went to the garden centre and found it almost deserted of customers. Forgetting her fatigue, she took a basket and lost herself for two hours wandering about between the rows of plants, examining each in turn, reading their labels, learning the French names, the Latin names, and trying to make sense of all the growing instructions. On this first visit, she bought some alliums, lavender, and a trowel, and spent a happy hour that afternoon clearing a small patch of a flower bed underneath the kitchen window. It felt good to plunge her hands into the moist black soil and dig little holes for the plants. Afterwards, she rested on her haunches and admired the dirt on her knees and under her fingernails. Ha! If only her husband could see her now, happy and dirty from her gardening!

A few days later, Laura shyly returned to the garden centre for a spade, a pair of gloves, and some lettuce and tomato plants. At the checkout, the girl asked her if she had a loyalty card and suggested that she buy a bag of compost and bottle of fertiliser. One thing led to another. Knowing nothing about horticulture, Laura found a bookshop and purchased several books on the subject. She also took copies of *Madame Bovary*, *Eugene Grandet*, and *Père Goriot* from the shelves.

'It's a long time since I sold copies of these. No one is interested in the classics anymore. The young ones, it's all about the internet.' The glamorous middle-aged shopkeeper casually scanned the books and pushed them back across the counter to Laura, tapping them at the last with her scarlet gel fingernails.

'It's a pity, all the same.' Almost tenderly, Laura picked up the books, cradling them to her heart.

Sitting in the front seat of her car with the books on her knees, she shivered, even though the day was warm. She thought of her mother and the terrible risk she had taken to hide her precious collection of French literature, banned by the state at the time. Laura's purchase took her back to her old home. After her father's release from prison, for some bizarre reason known only to the Party, he had been re-allocated their old tiny apartment. The decrepit block in the former French concession of the city had been condemned; perhaps it was part of the punishment, to make him live his lonely final days with the ghost of his wife, on the assumption that he would not last until the bulldozers moved in.

Laura had been in her final year at school and, having been informed of his release, she had taken the train to see him. She had found him down on his hands and knees in the corner of the apartment, emaciated, unshaven, in cheap black canvas slippers, a shadow of his former self. They said he was her father, but she had been so young when they sent her away to school that she had barely recognised him. And now, seeing him like this after all these years, part of her had been ashamed of him. He resembled a peasant, unwashed and smelling of cheap tobacco and with a faint aroma of urine. No one would think that he had once been a handsome, highly educated, athletic man. But that was what happened to enemies of the Party. Detention smashed them, broke their minds.

Breathing hard, her father was easing up a floorboard with a screwdriver that had been under a cupboard in the corner of the room.

'Baba, let me help, please.'

But he had dismissed her with a growl and an impatient wave of his hand. She watched him put his right ear to the floor, listen a while, then reach into the space under the boards. Triumphantly, he pulled out two packages, each carefully wrapped in brown paper and tied with string.

'Here they are! Mama's books. I kept them for you.' For a few seconds his cataract-clouded eyes seemed to twinkle with joy at his small victory'.

Laura had sat down cross-legged at his side as he untied the string. But the humidity had got to the books, and the pages were brown and rotting with mildew. Coughing with the dust, her father insisted on opening all the books, one by one, tears pouring down his stubbly cheeks. Laura rocked him in her arms as if she were the mother and he the child.

Only her mother's French bible and *Père Goriot* could be saved. After all Baba had been through, she now knew that was the day that killed him. He had died barely six weeks later, and she had had the books cremated with him. She had never told him that she had found out who her real father was. What would have been the point?

In Le Saut, spring rolled onwards, the temperature ratcheting up with each passing day. Out of Laura's lethargy and pain, a routine emerged. She got up early and did her exercises before taking her dog for a walk up the narrow track behind the house and into the woods along the hill top. If the weather was warm, she lazed in the sun, and in the afternoons she would potter about in the garden, clearing, digging, planting and generally tidying up.

She also arranged a broadband connection and VPN. Heart in her mouth, she had logged in for the first time since leaving Portugal and checked her private email She used the address for business and banking purposes, and it was known only to a chosen few. The blood had rushed to her head with relief. The inbox was empty. That evening, she was relaxed enough to log-in again and buy a sofa and a beautiful boat bed on the internet.

Every third day, she drove to the supermarket. Food was the one area where she struggled. It ought to have been a joy to be free to eat what she wanted again and not have her husband control every aspect of her diet, exercise and weight. It wasn't that she did not know how to cook, and she certainly missed the food of her homeland. It was more that she didn't seem to have the energy to put together more than an omelette with spring onions or a piece of steamed fish. She thought perhaps if she had a new kitchen fitted, it would make the task of producing a meal easier. The estate agent had given her a list of three local contractors. She had telephoned umpteen times, left messages, but always the response, if she got one, was the same.

'The House at the Foot of the Church? Well, yes, I know it. Of course. But Madame must understand, we're very busy at the moment. Next month, if you insist, perhaps I could pop by'.

Laura revelled in her solitude. She had no desire to fill the silence with music, radio or television, no need to socialise. Sometimes a noise would make her jump, a pigeon landing on the windowsill, the clatter of a distant lawnmower. She had always had to share space with others, never lived without supervision or surveillance, and never owned a home of her own before. Privacy was a rare luxury in her own country; if it existed at all, it was in the deepest recesses of people's hearts and minds. Laura enjoyed the evenings most, curling up with her books and her iPad on the sofa. She worked through each word, each line, each paragraph of *Père Goriot* with utmost patience, fascinated by the long descriptions and words for old-fashioned things. She had a photographic memory but made lists of the unfamiliar with notes in her own language to follow up obscure references with further investigation. There was peace in the focus, and it brought her closer to the dream of France that her mother had bequeathed to her and which, miraculously, Laura had held onto all these years. She gave herself permission to do nothing but sit in silence with the dog, listening to the falling night. Nights had always been the worst for her. That's when he used to come for her. But strangely, in this place, there were moments when she realised with relief that she didn't need to be afraid.

One Sunday morning, Laura went to the market in the nearest small town. Arriving early, she bought a pain au chocolat from the boulangerie and took a seat at a table in the sunshine outside a café overlooking the Loire. She was aware that the dog could be unpredictable around people and might growl or snarl at their ankles. Fortunately, there was only one other customer in the café, a lady of about sixty, her grey hair pulled back into a bun. She sat in a corner in the shade, but Laura noticed her because she was drinking a glass of white wine and had a pink walking stick decorated with silver stars.

How odd to drink wine for breakfast, Laura thought. But, feeling curious, she asked the waiter for a glass of the same.

'Dry or medium dry?'

'Which do you recommend?'

'That depends on one's personal preference, Madame,' he said, with a degree of disdain that she suspected was reserved for tourists.

'Medium dry', she replied, matching his hauteur with perfect French and a well- practised sniff and flick of her wild curls. Two could play at that game.

Stretching out her long legs, Laura watched the broad expanse of the river in the distance as it meandered between the sandbanks, blue as the sky, the surface gently wrinkled like an old face. A few geese glided around a little flat-bottomed houseboat that was moored to the bank, and a hazy three-quarter moon had hung around into the day. All was still, the only breeze the whisper of bird wings as they flew overhead. Such a peaceful scene.

Laura's thoughts turned to the artist, her artist. He would have loved to paint the scene before her. She wondered how he was getting on in Canada. His daughter must be… how old? University age at least. Laura sighed. Such a sweet child. In the early days, before they had got wise, Laura used to go round to the artist's tiny flat to pick up her commissions. She remembered a little girl prancing on the bed and showing off by naming all the countries of the world, in English from a wall map marked with coloured pins. It was all so long ago.

She nibbled her croissant out of the brown paper bag. She was not sure about the wine at first. It was rather bitter for breakfast, but the more she sipped, the more her toes tingled, the better it got. Turning her head, she looked back across the colourful awnings of the little market in the square. She admired the over-grand nineteenth-century town hall with its red, white and blue tricolour hanging limp around the flagpole, and she loved the old stone houses, a few of them half-timbered and decorated with flowerpots. Towering above everything at the top of the hill were the ramshackle ramparts and Rapunzel tower of the town's tatty château. Lifting her face to the sun, she found herself wondering whether she really was in this picture-postcard place. Was she dreaming? Or was it, perhaps, that her previous life had been the dream? If she reached out her finger into the day, would the bubble pop? France was not her country, its language, history and culture not her own, yet might she be able to rest safely in this valley where time was cherished? That morning, she felt at ease, happy almost, as if destiny had brought her full circle. For the first time ever, she was living life on her own terms.

One thing that caused her some disquiet, however, were the churches. Every village and town had one, even her own tiny Saut de Lion; there was no escaping them. On the one hand, she was afraid of what they stood for, the madness of faith and the price it exacted. On the other, the sound of their bells and their very presence brought her comfort, reminding her of her childhood home. Perhaps that was why she had bought the old house, so that she could rest once more in the shadow of a church, die there, if it came to that. At the same time, the idea of organised faith or religion in any form filled her with fury, her mind raging with contradictory thoughts and emotions that could not be ordered or rationalised. It would have been better if she had not been told, if she had never known. Did people think that sharing such things was kind? Laura had stood many times on different church thresholds, taken a deep breath and almost, almost pushed the heavy wooden doors open and gone in. At such moments she was a little girl again, her warm hand safe in that of her mother. Laura had hesitated on the steps of Hong Kong Cathedral shortly before her flight, loitered in Lisbon, dithered in New York, wavered in London, and last week she had stood for a whole two minutes in the timber porch of the little medieval church in Le Saut. But when the priest had emerged in his long black cassock, she had turned tail and scuttled away.

By ten o'clock, people were arriving for the Sunday market, battling with gestures and horn-honking for parking spaces all along the banks of the river. Most were walking down to the quay, where a huge banner showed the location of the Marché aux Puces.

Laura did not fully understand what the banner was indicating, but after paying the café bill, she followed a mother and grandmother navigating a pushchair down to the quay.

Along the banks of the river, as far as the eye could see, antiques and bric-a-brac had been set up on stalls or laid out on cotton sheets on the ground. It was as if the contents of all the houses, attics, barns and garages of the region had been poured out on the side of the cobbled quay. Laura was entranced. Her own country had destroyed the old; it had been smashed on the streets, purged and obliterated in people's minds. So much had been lost. It was easiest to forget, not to look back, for to do so would be to court insanity. Focus on the future, chase the new, that had been the way; start a business, buy a car, a flat-screen TV, an Italian leather sofa, a Louis Vuitton handbag. Now, in better years, people were trying to remember and reconstruct the long-forgotten rituals and prayers, but they were crude and disjointed. How like herself, she thought, a puppet trying to learn to move after the strings had been cut.

Stall after stall, Laura could not help herself. Reverently, she laid her fingertips on the old, touching, stroking, wondering; the carved arms of shabby antique chairs, the oxidised silver of a mirror, the tip of the needle on an old gramophone, the bell of a hunting horn glistening in the sun, curled like a snake in a velvet-lined box. Next to the horn sat a Victorian doll with a delicate porcelain face and matted long blonde hair, dressed in a tatty navy dress and cotton bonnet.

'May I?' Laura asked the stall-holder.

'Of course, Madame. She's German, early twentieth century.'

Tenderly and using both hands, Laura picked up the doll. Its blue glass eyes somehow blinked in recognition, as if to say hello, and Laura was smitten. Without hesitation, she bought the doll for ten euros. When she was a child, no one had toys, and a doll! That would have been beyond her wildest dreams!

'You'll have to choose a name for her'. The portly, moustached stall-holder grinned as he counted out her change, sensing his customer's satisfaction.

'Emilie. It was my mother's name.' It was indeed her mother's French name, but Laura had not known it until after her mother's death, when she had discovered it printed neatly in the front of her half-rotten, banned foreign books.

CHAPTER 7

One morning, a few weeks after Laura's arrival in the village, Father Michael was out for his early-morning run. It was a long-established discipline which had served as a form of meditation or solitary morning prayer. He never missed a day, come rain, snow, scorching heat, plagues of mosquitoes or, he recalled, even sniper's bullets.

He left through a crumbling wooden gate at the back of the presbytery, making a mental note to give it at least a lick of paint. He jogged gently around the back of the houses and up through the fields, towards the woods. It was a chill, misty morning and the birds seemed tardy, their song muted and sporadic. Father Michael's route varied only slightly, with an assortment of extensions or short-cuts, depending on the amount of time he had before his duties commenced. His knees ached as he puffed up the hill towards the wood, but he pushed on, anticipating the moment when the trees would swallow him up. There was a magic in the woods as the joy of entering or emerging slowly changed in response to the changing seasons. That morning the woods were several degrees colder than he had anticipated, the chill of the night air not yet gone. Rain had softened the ground to leave it damp beneath the priest's feet so that he ran with a soft squelch. Some of the leaves, like tiny cups and plates, held out water as he passed. Father Michael increased his pace, pushing himself into a sprint until he felt his heart thumping hard against his ribs. Into his sixties he might be, but he had been a wild young man and still liked to test himself, although he no longer punished himself for his shortcomings and failures, or so he thought.

After a few kilometres, there was a spot on the hill where a break in the trees gave a view of the village nestling in the valley below. There, Father Michael stopped to catch his breath. In winter he would sometimes watch the lights come on in the houses of his parishioners. Madame Rossignol's bedroom light at the far end of the village illuminated first, followed almost immediately by that of Old Santelli at the bottom of the street. As the minutes passed, other lights would come on, forming a silver chain between the residences of the village's two arch enemies. Such was the animosity between them that no one could remember the last time Madame Rossignol and Old Santelli had spoken to each other. Father Michael stood; panting, his hands on his hips, listening to the birds now scribbling songs enthusiastically on the new day, watching the sun coax its way through the clouds.

It was then that it happened; an inexplicable sensation of mind melting into itself and simultaneously exploding, a joyous yet terrifying falling away.

Awestruck, he watched as something or somebody slowly formed out of the morning mist and bubble of bird-song. His instinct was to fall to his knees, but he could not move. The shape was in the no-man's land between the sunflower fields and the forest. Slowly, the image metamorphosed as it emerged out of the silver-green spring leaves and soft sunlight; a translucent girl of seven or eight years old with long black hair, tiptoeing over the dandelions and daisies. What on earth was she doing out there alone at six-thirty in the morning? It was not someone he recognised, and he thought she must be lost. The breeze rustled in the trees, and the child began to dance as if it were she who was creating the day; light as a feather, fairy-like, spinning pirouettes and flying arabesques. Arms outstretched, she flung back her head, her neck, white, vulnerable, and exposed as she flew up to the sky.

Suddenly, somewhere a dog barked. Céline from the bar was walking her Alsatian up the field path. Startled by the sound, the girl's form crumpled and faded. At the last moment, she turned towards Father Michael, pleading with large eyes that were black as coal.

If this had been a one-off, perhaps Father Michael could have ignored the experience. But that was not the end of it. A few days later, the child returned to him. She had ventured down from the hill into the church. The sunlight was streaming in through the west window. Sensing someone enter during Mass, Father Michael looked to the back of the church and saw the luminescent, silver-green child wearing a straw hat and carrying a bunch of poppies in her hand.

He was struck dumb leaving his bewildered parishioners to stumble through the rest of the prayers without him. The girl had those same pleading oriental black eyes, except this time she was not dancing; she was waiting for something or someone. The brightness of the light from the window hurt the priest's eyes and he looked away. A few seconds later when he had the courage to look again, the child was gone.

At the end of Mass, he asked the tiny congregation if any of them had seen a child wander in towards the end of the service. They shook their heads, and Madame Rossignol and Madame Mini clucked and fussed about him like old hens.

'Are you alright, Father?' Are you sure? You look as if you've seen a ghost.'

'Are you eating properly? Are you sure? Rest up a little, take it easy.'

After his congregation had left, Father Michael went to the back of the church to investigate. All was just as it should be, except that someone had left a bunch of flowers tied with string on the step by the font. Stranger still, when he left the church there was a tall figure loitering in the shadows of the porch. But when the person saw the priest, he or she scuttled away.

That evening Father Michael took refuge in his study with his trombone, a collection of jazz records and CDs, and a large glass of cognac. The day had turned out to be a hot one, and he had been relieved to remove his habit and dog collar and fling them on the sofa. He flopped in an arm-chair, top shirt buttons opened, feet up on the coffee table, listening to François Guin's Four Bones smooching out a baleful 'East St Louis Toodle Oo'.

God knew that Father Michael was weary, mighty weary. The trial of the former bishop of the diocese was due to start. The man had been charged with child abuse; a series of incidents dating back decades that, it was alleged, the Church had covered up. Father Michael shuddered. How could he have been so naïve as to have been taken in by this man, his spiritual leader, his boss? The village priest abhorred politics in any form. As a boy, he had grown up at the centre of a web of lies, hypocrisy and fetid corruption. Wherever he had gone in the world, he had been able to smell it out; the news conferences, meetings and top-secret briefings. Gilded words out of the mouths of suave, over-confident, weak so-called wise men; the double-speak, half-truths, compromises and betrayal that had cost his men's lives and put innocents in mass graves with bullets in their heads. By the time Michael had come forward for the priesthood, he was middle-aged and had no ambition to climb the Church hierarchy. He was content to serve God as a hard-working parish priest, initially in some rough suburbs of Paris and Tours and latterly in the rural idyll of Le Saut de Lion. It had even been the bishop himself who had suggested his current parish to Father Michael.

'A change will do you good, my son. God knows, you've done more than enough on the front line.' They had been sitting in the bishop's lounge. The man had poured them each a coffee from a steaming, silver cafetière on a small table. Picking up his cup, the bishop had brushed back his long fringe and leaned nonchalantly back in his chair.

Father Michael had been aware of the rumours emerging at that time about the bishop, but it was now evident that, he, like many others, had been taken in by the man's quiet charisma and given the rumours no credence. But the scandal was out, and the media were baying for blood. Father Michael tried to keep an open mind, but doubts preyed at night and often he could not sleep. He thought about the appointment of the bishop; a man of great compassion and a brilliant theologian, tipped as one to watch – or so they had said.

'Who knows? He might go all the way and be a future Holy Father.'

But the truth was, 'brilliant theologian' was code for 'ultra conservative', the type that advocated the Latin Mass and was moving the French Church back to the right. The village priest abhorred such tendencies. They terrified him.

He was in reflective mood as he sipped his brandy, and his spirits sank as he listened to the familiar jazz trombones. He was finding it difficult to escape the conclusion that he had allowed himself to be marginalised by taking a position in a rural parish. Had he really chosen to look the other way and focus on the concerns of the vignerons, bakers, hoteliers, café owners, builders, plumbers, farmers, teachers, firemen and assorted others in his parish? None of them saints, for sure, but at least they called a spade a spade.

Father Michael swirled the cognac in his glass as if he might find an answer to his troubles there. What about the mysterious girl who had appeared to him? He was an old friend of the angels. As a child he had had an imaginary friend whom he called 'Golden Boy'. The boy appeared to him as an angel of his own age with wings. He was as real to the young Father Michael as the next boy, but the adults shook their heads and discouraged him from talking about the child who was his constant companion. So Father Michael had learnt long ago never to mention angels. Like most institutional religions, his Church was deeply suspicious of mavericks and mystics. At best, people would have thought him an oddball: at worst, he might have been classified as schizophrenic. But why should these visions return now? As a reminder or a warning?

He rested his head on the back of the chair and retreated into the pictures on the inside of his eyes. The swords of materialism were drawn against those of idealism in his mind. Why couldn't he see the world like others in the modern age? It was an old battle within him, but that night he was too used-up to engage with it. He finished his brandy and went to close the shutters. As for the visions, he dismissed them. He was upset, worried and over-tired: they were probably just a trick of the light.

CHAPTER 8

'Keeps herself to herself. I've seen her once or twice in the square, but she never comes in here.' So said Céline Duguet as she arranged herself and her copious cleavage next to Maddy and Madame Mini at the table in her café. It was early and they were waiting for Madame Rossignol to arrive before opening a meeting of the village church's Eight-Hundredth Anniversary Committee. The tapestry was its flagship project.

'How old is she, the newcomer? Anyone with her, husband, children?' Maddy enquired, tipping two sachets of sugar into her espresso.

'Impossible to tell. She always seems to wear a hat or scarf, and sunglasses. Not young, and she seems to be quite alone apart from a dog. She was up on the hill with it the other day.'

'I saw her at the market. The strangest thing, she was buying cherries and cradling an antique doll in her arms.'

The conversation ticked on as if the stranger were a rare bird or endangered beast and the women were vying to declare sightings.

The tardy final member of their party, Madame Rossignol, was, as she herself would say, never late but never early. Knowing this, Céline lit up, puffed the smoke backwards and upwards and held the cigarette elegantly out into the street so that her friends did not have to inhale the smoke. She didn't give a fig for no-smoking legislation. Who was there to enforce it, anyway, if she, the propriétaire, did not?

'Young Santelli says he saw her in Super U, and Jeanne in the boulangerie told me that she likes pain au chocolat, and a baguette, and she loves strawberry ice cream, two scoops. She speaks the strangest French apparently, very slow, correct and precise, like an old-fashioned newsreader, subjunctives and all. Très chic!' Céline fluttered her false eyelashes at her companions, who laughed.

'Bravo for subjunctives!' The English-woman raised her coffee cup in mock salute to her friend. You had to hand it to Céline. Not only was she an expert in taking others down a peg or two, but she knew how to laugh at herself. If truth be told, Maddy, like most of the village ladies, had not liked Céline one bit when she had taken up with Henri Duguet. Divorced twice, brassy, blunt, straight-talking, she was a poorly educated girl from Lyon who, in her younger days, had modelled her looks on an unlikely mix of Pamela Anderson and Brigitte Bardot. The trouble was that three children and three decades later, with her dyed and impeccable back-combed blonde locks, pouting pink lips and a chest extension, the look was not quite what it had once been. Not that the men seemed to mind, with all eyes on her blouse-popping bosom that caused them to flock to her bar. If they got too familiar, she would cut them off at the knees with a sharp riposte, and if they drank too much, she would refuse to serve them and send them home to their wives with a flea in their ear.

But the thing about Céline was that she cared. She was interested in people, and kind. She had time for everyone.

'How's Jean's leg? What did the vet say about the dog?

Or, 'Don't worry about that! I'll drive you to the hospital for your check-up. Yes, and wait for you. No, no trouble at all.'

In time, folk forgot about her accent and poor grammar, especially her failure to make use of the subjunctive mood. And so, after a couple of years, Céline had been accepted into the community. The men were reconciled to the new-look café, even if it did bring in women and passing foreigners. And Maddy, Madame Mini and Madame Rossignol would be the first to admit that Céline was a mover and shaker in the tapestry initiative. She had bullied, cajoled, and enticed even the most reluctant villagers into weaving a few square centimetres. 'All the names of those who give their time will be up on a plaque in the church. Be a shame to miss out, don't you think?'

Madame Mini broke a large piece off her croissant, popped it into her mouth and washed it down with a noisy gulp of espresso.

Céline continued on the subject of the newcomer. 'All the same, it's a shame about the House at the Foot of the Church.'

At the mention of the house, the other two women had drawn back, like cats at the edge of a river. What were they so afraid of Maddy wondered? Falling in, or what might be reflected back? But she had learnt to leave well alone. Every family had its secrets.

'I mean, what if that poor woman, all alone down there, wants anything sorting?' That was quite an admission coming from Céline, because whenever anyone needed a job doing, she always knew a man who could fix a broken shutter, clear a gutter, fit a bathroom, unblock a drain, or do whatever might be needed.

'Pfff! It's completely ridiculous, after all these years.' Whenever the taciturn Madame Mini interrupted a conversation, she would be curt and to the point. 'High time people let bygones be bygones.'

'Yes, it's complicated. Always has been.' Céline frowned and wafted cigarette smoke this way and that into the street as if she were directing contraflow traffic. 'My own grandmother, God bless her soul, she was a widow with two small children to feed. What was she supposed to do during the Occupation? Let them starve? So, what if she did sleep with a German officer? Actually, he was a kind man, and my grandma helped lots of neighbours with extra bits of meat, milk or eggs. Never took any money for it, unlike others, but after the war, well…' She made an explosive sound with her bright pink lips and waved her hand in a motion that suggested decapitation. 'Hypocrites! Grandma was just as much a patriot as the next person. I ask you, who are we to judge? Who knows the choices we would have made in the same circumstances? You don't survive a war, starvation and tyranny by being *nice*.' Viciously, Céline spat her last word, then shrugged and stubbed out her cigarette in an ashtray she kept hidden behind the bar for her own use.

Maddy took a sharp intake of breath. Normally the subject of wartime collaboration was taboo in the village, and certainly not mentioned in the presence of outsiders. It occurred to her that despite the depressing subject matter, it was in fact a back-handed compliment to her, for they had forgotten that she, La Folle Anglaise, was, as people frequently said, not from round here.

At that moment, they saw Madame Rossignol processing

slowly across the cobbles towards them, and all judged it prudent to let matters rest.

All the same, Maddy thought, perhaps she would pay the newcomer a visit. Poor soul, she probably had no idea of the history of the place. Best not to mention it, of course. Why burden her with the past?

CHAPTER 9

'Hello! It's just me.'

Laura was on her knees weeding her vegetable garden in front of the kitchen. Where was the dog when she needed him? She had bought him as a guard. In a flash, she was up on her feet, gripping the trowel like a knife. Best to strike first. But the sun was in the other's eyes, and she was oblivious to Laura's terror. A stately galleon of a woman in imperial purple linen sailed across the gravel drive and wobbled down the steps to the kitchen patio. It was then that the stranger saw not Laura ready to kill, but something else.

It was late afternoon and still hot. Laura had left the kitchen window and door shutters wide open. The stranger hesitated, her jaw dropping dumpling-like into the thick folds of her neck. It was all there on display. The door hanging off the old kitchen cupboard, and on the camping table in the middle of the room the piles of half-empty food packets, cornflakes, biscuits, crisp packets, bags of fruit, takeaway containers, dirty wine glasses and Laura's single plate and cup, unwashed from lunch. She would rinse them later in the evening when she needed them. But if you had asked her then what she planned to eat, she would have had no idea; she ate what she could put together at the time.

The woman frowned, concerned, and then conjured a broad, generous smile, that suggested all was forgiven. 'Maddy,' she said, proffering her pudgy, suntanned hand. 'I just thought I'd drop in and introduce myself. Welcome to Le Saut'.

'Enchantée, Laura de Silva.' Laura removed her gardening gloves and forced a polite response. Her hands were wet with sweat. Looking as innocent as heaven, with not an evil thought in his head, the dog appeared at the kitchen door. Laura pursed her lips. He would growl and snap at strangers in the market to the point that she no longer took him into town, but he was evidently useless as a guard dog.

'What a beautiful house! The woman turned to survey the garden. 'Do you speak English?'

'Yes, but I am more comfortable in French.' The cogs in Laura's mind grated with the effort of switching languages and of making small talk. She had been alone for months, talking to people only when she was arranging things or making a purchase.

'That's probably a good thing. I'm English, but I've been living in France for thirty years and more. My daughter says I don't speak either language properly any more. Listen, I've got a beef hot-pot on. Why don't you come and have a bowl with me?' Maddy's bright blue eyes drifted briefly back to the evidence of Laura's vulnerability, the decrepit pre-war kitchen and the debris all over the camping table. 'It's no fun, eating alone. Do say yes. As-tu faim?'

Laura's heart missed a beat. She hadn't been expecting this; she was caught off guard, completely disarmed. One word, one simple word, that's all it took. The smell of lavender, a tingling sensation, blood rushed to her head and she felt weak at the knees.

'Are you alright?'

There it was again. Tu, thou, you, the stranger's subtle switch from the formal 'vous' to the more informal, intimate 'tu'. Such a simple change, but it reached out across the years, lassoing deep memories of stories, songs, and echoes of prayers neither remembered nor forgotten. They were prayers that had been whispered in the shadows of the night when they could not be overheard, for in those days even one's own son or daughter could not be trusted. Any child might make a slip and betray you. In that moment, with that word, it was as if Laura's mother herself had put her arms around her and pulled her close. The smell of lavender and coal smoke and the unforgettable scent of those who belonged to her, of being snuggled up under the old red duvet with Mama and Baba. 'Tu', a word that promised family and home and that all would be well.

Almost before she knew it, Laura was accompanying Maddy up the steep lane into the village. Never in her life had she been so close to someone who was so overweight. Maddy's thighs were so large that she waddled like a duck, puffing and panting, but chattering all the time. Laura struggled to keep up, not with her companion's pace, although she did walk surprisingly fast, but the speed with which words tumbled out of her mouth. The torrent of unfamiliar vocabulary was compounded by Maddy's English accent and hilarious cross-cultural mélange of gestures and facial expressions.

The three-storey building just off the village square was adorned with signs and accreditation plaques with a myriad of stars and rosettes.

Chambres d'Hôte
Antiquitiés

Crème Thé Anglais
Café, Gâteaux

'This is me!' Maddy wiped the sweat from her brow with the back of her hand and slipped the key into the lock. Idly, Laura wondered how the woman would cope with a hot summer.

Laura had noticed the house before; you couldn't miss it. Outside were three small white painted wrought-iron tables and chairs, flowerpots, a stone lion and a small wooden windmill. The kitchen at the back was minimalist and ultra-modern, in cream and white, with elegant French windows opening to a small garden behind. A rich, winey, meaty smell made her stomach rumble.

'Come in. Sit down.' Maddy slipped on a pair of gloves and pulled a large brown casserole dish from the oven. 'I don't have any bed and breakfast guests in at the moment, so it's just you and me.'

'Can I help you with something?' Laura felt uncomfortable, even anxious, using the 'tu' form. But what was there to be anxious about? What ulterior motive could the crazy Englishwoman have for inviting her for supper, and what harm could possibly come to her here in France?

Soon the large table by the window was set; two knives, two spoons, a baguette, a jug of water, glasses and a bottle of red wine. The hot-pot had thick, rich gravy with carrots, little onions, celery and chunks of tender beef. It could have been improved by the addition of some fresh chilli, Laura thought; even so, she had to admit to herself that it was a long time since she had tasted anything so delicious. She would have wolfed the whole bowl down if good manners had not restrained her. Sensing her guest's appreciation, Maddy cut more baguette and offered her a large chunk, pushing the butter dish towards her.

'Help yourself.' Another 'tu'. Each time the tiny word was used, Laura softened a little more inside. She tried to resist, but the good home-made food and the company made her realise how much she had been neglecting herself and how isolated she had become. She watched Maddy eat, dipping little pieces of bread into her stew.

'Santé!' Maddy raised her wine glass. She was, Laura thought, surprisingly beautiful in her own way. Impeccably turned out, although everything about her was dramatic. Her purple linen trousers and matching tunic were only slightly creased, her nails and lips were a cheery cherry red, and a large turquoise ethnic bead necklace hung around her neck. Her grey hair was cut in a short, snappy crop which drew attention to her sparkling blue eyes and happy face with its two sweet dimples, one nestled in the folds of each cheek. It was an innocent face, an honest face.

At the same time, her husband's voice boomed in her head. 'Westerners, fat, soft, spoilt! But their time has come. The Motherland is on the rise!'

Laura marvelled at her host's naïve openness. It was a rare thing, in her experience. In some strange way she felt sorry for her, and this made Laura want to protect her, as if Maddy, not she herself, were the vulnerable one. This was surely the impression her host had got on seeing the mess in Laura's kitchen. Laura was a little ashamed at this thought. It had been more than a relief to give up her weekly facials and stringent gym routine, and to abandon her designer clothes. Unconsciously, she put her hand to the top of her head. She had decided to stop dyeing her hair, too, but the root growth had now reached a point where a broad white streak ran badger-like down her parting.

'So, Laura, what brought you to Le Saut, and to that house?'

Laura summoned all her professional skill to force a large smile before waving her left hand graciously towards the church spire that could be seen towering beyond the end of the garden. If the answer was a prepared one, it was no less true.

'The Loire and the Touraine are the heart of France. So much history, culture and beauty all in one place, and I love Balzac!' That usually worked to satisfy people, to shut them up.

'Ah, Balzac. A very unconventional man. The French Dickens, they call him. What's your favourite work? I like *Eugene Grandet*.'

'Mine's *Père Goriot*.' Judging attack to be the best form of defence, Laura moved on quickly. 'And what brought you to France, might I ask?' Unconsciously she had slipped back to the 'vous' form, but Maddy was unfazed.

'The usual, my dear! L'amour!' She chuckled. 'I fell in love with a tall, dark, handsome Frenchman. We married and had a son and a daughter. Sadly, my husband, Antoine, is no longer with us.'

'I'm sorry to hear that.'

Maddy smiled, sat back in her chair and folded her arms on the shelf of her stomach. She still wore her wedding ring.

'I have my children and three grandchildren. My son lives in Paris and my daughter in London. We see each other three or four times a year, so life is good. I'm blessed. More hotpot?' Barely had Laura nodded her head than Maddy was ladling another large spoonful into her guest's bowl.

There was a pause, and the two women ate in silence. Laura anticipated the next question; the one about her own family, the one she dreaded. Best to take the initiative again and get it over with.

'I'm divorced. No children. I never wanted any'. Laura lied, quickly, efficiently, looking Maddy in the eye. But she felt uncomfortable. Why? It was such a long time since she had told the truth about anything. Why should such a tiny lie bother her now? But she knew why. This woman was not like her husband's friends with their fat pockets and tiny, calculating eyes, always scouting for opportunities, looking for prey, sly, and ready to pounce. Wild dogs, every one of them, clever, sophisticated, international ones adorned with all the trappings of modernity, pretending to be harmless and likeable. No, Maddy was not at all like that. She was the product of a gentler world. She was genuine. She was kind.

Yet again, Laura judged attack to be the best form of defence and deftly changed the subject.

'Such a beautiful kitchen'. Again she conjured her best stage smile, and then said confidentially, leaning forward. 'Actually, I want to get a new kitchen installed at my house but I'm having trouble finding someone to do the work.'

There was a pause in Maddy's response, just a short intake of breath, almost imperceptible, but it was enough to warn Laura that something was wrong. She hesitated, but calculating that she had nothing to lose, decided to push on.

'The estate agent recommended various local contractors, but I telephoned several people and none of them got back to me.' Laura tried not to sound desperate.

'Oh, my dear! This is rural France, country people, you know. They are ready when they are ready, in their own time!' Maddy's response was too quick and too jovial, and Laura saw right through it. She had grown up in an environment of rumour and counter-rumour, backstabbing and betrayal. She had a sixth sense, and it told her now that she had tripped a wire, gone too far.

'Perhaps they don't like foreigners?' Laura backtracked, raising her elbows to gesture dramatically with her face and eyes, trying to make a joke out of her appearance.

'No, it's not that. The French are a complicated lot! Believe me, I've been living in this country over thirty years. Let me reassure you, it's nothing to do with you, my dear.' Slowly Maddy folded her napkin, giving herself time to think. 'I think Victor will be coming soon. He normally visits at this time of year. He fitted my kitchen for me. Normally the locals don't like it when people from outside the region come in and take their work. But they make an exception for Victor. He's a strange one, but harmless enough, poor soul. Don't you worry. I'll speak to Father Michael and see what we can sort out. Eat up now! After dinner I'll take you to meet some people. No, not at all. I insist.'

CHAPTER 10

No one looked up as the two women entered, and Laura was grateful for that. It crossed her mind that she ought to remove her shoes, as if she were entering a home or a temple. She had never seen anything quite like it; six people all sitting quietly in front of looms in a high-roofed, timber-framed barn. They were lost in concentration, hands moving, threading, tugging, softly hammering, turning the levers at the top of the looms. It was as if each were playing their own part in a muffled symphony. Her eyes were drawn to the far wall where a series of sixteen pictures were displayed, four for each season of the year. The members of the quartets each had a different picture or motif corresponding to village life at the relevant time of year, and each was characterised by its own colour scheme. This meant that the four pictures representing each season came together as one. The effect was to create a stunning large-scale piece of art.

After dinner, Laura had been sleepy and had not been keen to venture out.

Maddy had smiled. 'Come on! You'll meet people. It will be fun.'

Fun! Laura's heart had sunk at the word, but soothed by the wine and hot food and not wanting to offend her host, she had acquiesced, although at the time she had not been entirely sure to what. Maddy's explanations in both French and English had been accompanied by a series of dramatic but absurd gestures that had looked as if she were conducting a comedy band. It was only when Laura was there that she could piece things together. The people were weaving the pictures in sections on their looms.

A floorboard creaked, and a woman of between sixty and seventy with grey hair in a bun emerged from behind a large wooden loom.

'Bienvenue! I have been expecting you'. The woman blinked rapidly as if emerging from a dark place and, smiling shyly, reached out to shake the newcomer's hand. Laura recognised her from the café on the day of the Marché aux Puces. A shiver ran down the back of her neck, a feeling that the encounter was in some way pre-ordained. Perhaps not quite everything had been left to chance?

'This is Madame Mini,' Maddy said. 'She's our Master and teacher. We could never have begun this project without her.'

'We are a team,' Madame Mini responded, twisting her hands in front of her in a gesture of humility. 'It's Maddy who is the true artist. It's she who painted the paintings in the first place, and then several of us came up with the idea of making them into tapestries to celebrate the eight-hundredth anniversary of the church. The plan is to complete four small panels in teams each season. We aim to finish them all for Easter, when we are going to hang them on the church walls. There will be a special service.'

Laura searched for an appropriate expression of approval and genuine amazement. 'Incroyable'. She deployed this dictionary-learnt word with aplomb, then, turning to Maddy, said almost accusingly, 'You didn't tell me you were an artist.'

'*Was* an artist.' Maddy shrugged. 'I haven't got the energy for it anymore.'

'But who are the workers?'

'Workers! You mean volunteers, or slaves.' Maddy laughed. 'Why, just us from the village. Many of us lend a hand, even the children. Some of them are our best weavers.'

'But isn't it a difficult art that requires training?'

Madame Mini bobbed a quaint little nod, acknowledging Laura's respect. 'One could be purist about it. All the great weavers have a different touch, a personal signature you might say, but with patience and perseverance, anyone can achieve a decent standard.'

Maddy picked up the conversation. 'Madame Mini trained at the great Gobelin tapestry House in Paris. She knows everything there is about tapestry making. Of course, we could never match the professionals at the Gobelin. But that doesn't stop us. Madame Mini guides and supervises. Truly, she is a saint! The miracle is that somehow or other we ham-fisted bunch of farmers and ignoramuses manage to muddle through. And we are improving. We have just finished the spring tableau.'

'Viens voir, Laura.' Ever so softly, ever so gently, Madame Mini intervened, guiding Laura by the elbow. For the second time that day she was disarmed by a simple word. It was as if Madame Mini knew her already, from somewhere before, a long time ago, but how could that be? No one had ever called her by her name before, not this name, not Laura. In Lisbon she had been Senhora de Silva. In France she'd mostly been just Madame.

With a whisper of weft deftly threaded through warp, Laura was drawn into the picture. Madame Mini's quiet explanations were hypnotic, and with a feather-like touch on her elbow, Laura was shuttled around the studio. The spring tapestry was laid out in a square on a large table in the corner of the studio. In the first two sections, trees on the hill were covered in white blossom, red and yellow flowers cheering jauntily in the window boxes. In the third section, the eye was drawn to the undulating turquoise blue of the awning outside the café bar with the shadows of people underneath. In the fourth stood the church against a backdrop of blue, and in the top left was a large white dove. It was a remarkable achievement for amateurs, Laura could see that; modern, abstract in design, yet with the artist's clever manipulation of perspective, it was medieval at the same time.

Madame Mini whispered so as not to disturb the weavers. 'We made a lot of mistakes at first and were constantly unpicking and remaking, but practice makes perfect. I am very proud of our work.'

Laura was shown a large paper with simplified tracings of the paintings. They had been modified for the tapestry. It was copies of these that provided the guidelines for the tapestry makers, laid behind the warp threads as a template.

'May I?'

'Of course.'

Laura reached out a finger and gently stroked across the weft of the tapestry, following some jaunty yellow threads.

'We've just started on summer.' Madame Mini explained as they moved behind a loom being operated by a well-dressed elderly lady sitting on two tatty cushions to give her the comfort and height she wanted. 'May I introduce Madame Rossignol? She's chair of our tapestry committee.'

The old lady nodded curtly and sniffed. Laura sensed immediately that this was a person of some stature and influence in the village. Fascinated, she watched Madame Rossignol's gnarled, suntanned fingers tenderly and deftly weaving threads of a golden yellow to fill in the petals of a sunflower. When she had finished the section, she stood by pulling herself up on the frame of the loom. 'Eh bon, that's my shift done. Time for refreshments.' She smiled politely to excuse herself.

'Would you like to have a turn?' Maddy asked. 'I'll sit with you and show you how. We can work on the lower section here. It's easier, just straight lines. Don't worry. You'll soon learn.'

***

Later that evening, Laura lay in bed, with the dog snoring gently in his basket in the corner of the room.

'Laura,' she said her name out loud, this way and that, experimenting with the pronunciation as if trying it on for size. She thought about the tapestry teacher, the rhythm of her words and old-fashioned French courtesies echoing in her mind. Weave, warp, weft, yarn, wool, cotton, repeat. Madame Mini spoke the language of her trade with tender reverence, like prayers. There was a gentle magic about her that bewitched.

But Laura could not rest. Her mind worried over the evening's events. Maddy and Madame Mini had offered her a welcome she did not deserve. And what on earth had possessed her? It had all happened in a moment. She had squeezed onto the bench in front of a loom with Maddy at her side, and the tapestry teacher had put a thread of red wool into her hand.

Soft, long, the colour of happiness, the colour of joy, the colour of blood. It was all too dangerous. Friends were weapons to be turned against you. People got hurt.

Rolling over in bed, Laura vowed not to get involved in village life. Best to keep things simple. That would be safest for all concerned.

She slept fitfully, half awake, half in a dream, her heart beating in time to the soft thump of Madame Mini's little wooden hammer on the wool. But someone else was pressing a ball of soft red wool into her hand. It was a peace offering from Little Swan.

She saw the other's face once more, remembered as a girl, soft and gentle, but already hardening with training and adult realities. They had met at boarding school, starting out as mutual competitors, but in the end Little Swan had become Laura's only real friend. Where Laura had curls, Little Swan had dimples, and the Director had liked them too. They had called each other sister, Laura the younger one, Little Swan the elder. The click of knitting needles joined the thump of the tapestry makers' hammers in Laura's mind. She was back in her school dormitory, snuggled up close to Little Swan for warmth. The air was acrid with smoke from the coal bricks that were burned in the winter; it would settle black around their nostrils while they slept. It was a winter Sunday afternoon, the only time in the week when there was no training. Heads together, sitting on the bottom bunk and wrapped up in their padded green jackets and woollen hats, they whispered as they knitted away their hatred, anger and pain. God knows how, but someone had smuggled in a picture of a skinny blonde American film star wearing pink leg warmer, and they were defiant in making copies of these. They couldn't get pink wool, but red was better. Of course, they never dared wear the completed articles, not as leg warmers, not until years later. But they had worn them as scarves, and because they were senior students they had got away with it when younger ones could not. A small victory in the face of tyranny and power. Laura rolled over in her sleep. She saw Little Swan on her death-bed, reaching out to hold her hand, smiling through the morphine, her face haggard beyond her years with cancer.

'Do not mourn me, little sister. When I am gone, you will be free. Go! Live! Do it for me!'

CHAPTER 11

Father Michael let the garden gate slam behind him, not caring if the noise woke the neighbours. He was in his running shorts and wasn't feeling charitable, not that morning. Leaving earlier than usual, he set off in double time up the hill for his morning run. His excuse was that he wanted to beat the heat, for it was warm already, but he knew he was really running away from the sense that he personally had failed. Witness testimonies in the trial of the bishop were emerging in the press: fractured middle-aged men with broken lives whose accounts were harrowing. They told how the man who had risen through the ranks of the clergy to bishop had sought them out, vulnerable misfits, orphans from children's homes – been kind to them with food and wine, then abused them in his own home.

Father Michael pushed himself up the hill. He did not care that his body needed time to warm up. Arms pumping at his side, heart thumping, lungs burning, he did not stop until he was at the top. Hands on his ribcage, he bent double, trying to catch his breath. When he stood up, there she was, walking out of the halo of the rising sun, wearing a red scarf among the thousands of black and yellow bobbing heads of the sunflowers. Stepping backwards, he shaded his eyes. For a brief moment it occurred to him that the angel was appearing to him again, but he instantly put this down to not sleeping well. Then he heard shouting and barking.

'Non! Non! Non!'

The woman was battling with a dog that she had let run on a long lead. She was trying to call him in, but he was running at full pelt and obviously stronger than she. It was the dog that brought the two of them together, tearing out of the field, hauling the woman behind him. A fierce, creamy-white animal of not insignificant size, he burst into the clearing at the top of the hill. Teeth bared, growling, ready for a fight, he squared up to Father Michael.

'Non!' the woman yelled.

Calmly, Father Michael reached out the palm of his left hand towards the dog. Man and dog stared at each other. Then, all at once, the dog stopped growling and began to wag its tail.

'Hush now, hush.'

The flustered woman, who had now arrived in the clearing, stared in astonishment.

Slowly, Father Michael approached the animal, palm outstretched, and the dog, who just a few seconds before had looked ready to tear him to pieces, sniffed at it and then licked his hand.

'Be careful,' the woman said, in beautifully precise if strangely accented French. 'I am so sorry. He is very...' he hesitated, searching for the word 'unpredictable'.

'So I see.' Not taking his eyes off the animal, Father Michael rested his hand on the top of the dog's head.

Addressing the animal, he said, 'What's your name?'

'Boris,' the woman replied with a laugh that tinkled through the cool early morning like a bell. 'He was a rescue dog from

Albania. It's the name he came with. He was on death row when I found him. They had given him a week to live. If no one came forward to take him within that time, they would have shot him.'

'He's a lucky one,' said Michael as he continued to stroke the dog.

'You have a magic touch.' Reeling in the slack from the lead, the woman came forward; then, unravelling herself sinuously, she squatted down on the opposite side of the dog to Father Michael. Tenderly, she placed her hand on Boris's back, and the two of them stroked the animal, who growled softly with pleasure. Laura's hands were tiny, her nails poorly cut and rough from gardening. She wore no wedding ring. As the animal's breathing deepened, the humans too relaxed, their hands moving in time to soothe the dog and, Father Michael thought, probably themselves.

'I've never seen him like this before with a stranger,' the woman whispered. 'He can be wild sometimes. That's why I never let him off the lead and keep him away from the village. No one quite knows what happened to him in his early life.'

Father Michael nodded, imagining the poor animal that at this moment was so tame, loitering around cafés and bars, begging for scraps, being kicked and beaten by drunks when he was in the wrong place at the wrong time. Then, for the first time ,the priest looked at the woman. He stared, and she stared back, completely unabashed, with large brown eyes. He struggled to decide whether she was Korean or Chinese or perhaps, as the man in the bar had said, Japanese. Her hair was tied back under a red silk scarf. This had come loose while she chased after the dog, and tiny curls of grey peeked out at the front. Without question she was beautiful, her skin smooth and softy browned like salted caramel, but at the same time there was something slightly odd about the way her features were put together: the size of her eyes, the height of her cheekbones, the angle of her jaw. A cool breeze blew through the soft blond hairs on Father Michael's bare legs. How could she know nothing about him and yet make him feel as if she saw right into his heart?

'Laura de Silva. I moved to the village a few months ago.' The woman lowered her eyes, smiled and offered him her hand.

'Michael,' he said, knowing at once that she was lying. Strange, he would think later, that he had seen through her disguise instantly but been completely taken in by the bishop. But in that moment, he felt awkward without his cassock, conscious of the smell of sweat and dog and the heat rising from the ground. He did not want to ruin the moment by telling her he was the village priest. Not yet, at least. But already he realised that she probably had him partially unmasked, for he recognised her from the way she moved. They had seen each other before. It was Laura who had been loitering in the shadows of the church porch that day. Was it she who had left the flowers by the font?

***

The following weekend, Father Michael was painting the gate in the presbytery garden. Originally, he had planned to leave the job for Victor, who was coming from Provence for his annual holiday at the end of the month. His friend needed to be kept busy. But that Saturday afternoon, Father Michael could not be still: his head thumped with memories of incoming mortars and an incessant background clatter of small arms fire. As he worked, he made long slow strokes of paint, following the grain of the wood. The sun beat down on his back, relaxing the tension in his shoulders, and the simplicity of the largely repetitive task calmed him. If only life were this straightforward.

So absorbed was the priest in his work that he did not hear him come. He was sitting there silently, in the shade, waiting, watching him with his coal-black eyes.

Only when Father Michael finally straightened his back and looked up did he see the dog, who gave him a soft 'woof' as if to say hello. 'Salut, Boris! What are you doing here? Where's your mistress?'

Stiffly, he got up and, wiping his hands on a rag, popped out into the street to look for Laura.

'So, you're here alone, are you?' he said after a while. The dog wagged its tail and seemed to give the priest a cheeky grin. 'Playing hooky? I'm not sure that's allowed. Thirsty?' He fetched Boris a bowl of water from the kitchen, which the animal lapped up greedily.

Such a strange-looking mongrel, Father Michael thought. Boris had a sharp, impish face, reminiscent of a fox's, he was of medium build and was covered in a sparse, coarse, creamy-white fur. Heaven knew what kind of cross the dog was. He looked like a scrawny, very poor relation of a Russian Samoyed though the priest could not imagine Boris herding anything.

Man and dog passed a happy half-hour together, the priest finishing the last couple of slats of the gate, the dog observing, lazing in the shade. At intervals Father Michael would look up and down the street for Laura. But there was still no sign of her. When he finished the painting, he decided he would take Boris home.

CHAPTER 12

Laura never understood why she asked Father Michael into the house that day. She put it down to fate. She knew that he'd realised she had not told the entire truth the other morning on the hillside when she gave him her name; she'd seen the flicker, almost imperceptible, in his bright blue eyes. The man was no fool. Perhaps she had issued the invitation because they had looked so mischievous, man and dog, standing there at her garden gate like naughty friends. Father Michael was dressed in faded blue workman's dungarees and a grey T-shirt, with streaks of blue paint on his forehead and around his temples. Perhaps the invitation to enter her house simply reflected her relief at seeing Boris. She had been looking for the dog everywhere. Perhaps it owed something to the fact that before Laura issued her invitation, they had spent over half an hour crashing about together through the brambles, trees and nettles around the boundary of her property, trying to find Boris's escape route.

'I'm sure I didn't leave the gate open. He must have got out somewhere.'

Laura had felt uncomfortable about drawing the stranger into the search, but the man did not seem to mind; on the contrary, he seemed to relish the opportunity. He was fit, energetic and agile, effortlessly moving heavy pieces of old stone to check for a breach in the wall.

Eventually they admitted defeat and retreated to the patio, laughing at the ludicrousness of their activity.

'That dog is a proper Houdini,' the priest joked with a shrug and a smile. He had a round face, almost pudgy but tough at the same time, with a large crooked nose that looked as if it had been broken at least once in the past. Apologising for the man's scratches and stings, Laura fetched a tube of anti-histamine cream, and the two of them shyly swapped it back and forth, dabbing it on their barbs and stings, while trying and failing to be cross with the errant dog. Her visitor's forearms were tanned and muscular, covered in fine, sun-bleached blond hair. Laura was tempted to reach out and stroke them, to disturb them this way and that. With all the activity, she forgot her suspicion of religion. Perhaps because the stocky, grey-haired man with bramble scratches on his forearms and blue paint on his face resembled a middle-aged clown. Perhaps because the afternoon was tipping into evening and loneliness had overpowered prudence. Whatever the reason, the invitation, when it came, had seemed the most natural thing in the world.

'May I offer you a cup of tea or coffee?' Another fine phrase from her French primer.

'Tea! That would be magnificent.' What a grand word for a cup of tea, Laura thought, as the priest stretched his back, and surveyed approvingly the garden with its view of the church spire.

'Please come in.'

Just like that, the two of them crossed the threshold into the living room. Suddenly, Laura remembered the painting, and shot a guarded glance towards it. The shutters were closed against the heat of the day, and it hung in shadow on the back wall.

'Black or green?' she asked quickly.

'Sorry?'

'The tea; black tea with milk, or green tea?'

He was caught halfway between removing his tatty old trainers and looking around the room. He wore no socks, and his feet were pale and square.

'Whatever you are having'. Again, his simple smile. 'May I help you?'

Before she knew it, he had followed her into the kitchen. Thankfully, it was tidier than the day when Maddy had called.

'No, really, it's fine.' Laura took a second mug from the one rickety shelf that managed to cling on to the wall. Out of the corner of her eye, she watched the priest. It was obvious that he had never been in the house and curiosity was getting the better of him. He had a cautious, expectant look on his face, as if waiting for something. Then it came, that microsecond of creaking silence, the same one Laura had experienced when the subject had arisen that day in Maddy's kitchen.

'Such a lovely house.' He made the same mistake they all did, rushing too quickly to fill the vacuum with platitudes. Laura nodded, turned her back to him and dropped a handful of green tea leaves in the bottom of a teapot, hoping that more might be revealed.

It wasn't. Too quickly, the priest changed the subject. 'Maddy mentioned you need help with a new kitchen?'

Slowly, not wishing to appear too keen, Laura turned to face him. 'Yes. As you can see, it is rather in need of a…',

She faltered, searching for the correct word, then remembered one she had seen on an advertisement in the hardware shop. 'A make-over.'

'Indeed!' But he did not smile. Now it was his turn to hesitate as he surveyed the situation, measuring up the room with his eyes, returning all the time to the door at the back of the kitchen that led to the cellar, then quickly looking away. What did he see there? Did he know about the ghosts, Laura wondered? She knew they were there: every time she went into the cellar, she felt their presence, and sometimes she heard their footsteps or their voices.

'I think we can sort something out.' The priest smiled now, brusquely squaring his shoulders. 'My friend Victor is coming soon. He likes to take on jobs, says it gives him peace. I'll speak to him when he arrives. He's an excellent carpenter.'

'A design similar to Maddy's would be perfect,' Laura said lightly, mimicking a phrase she often heard the ladies in the village use. 'I would pay him well. But will that be alright? I presume he is from outside the region? I don't want trouble.' She trod carefully, tactfully employing phrases she had picked up from gossip overhead at the boulangerie and village shop.

'Don't worry about that. Céline Duguet is a veritable Madame Fix-It. She's brokered a priority arrangement for Victor. Let's say he makes a contribution to parish funds.'

They returned to the living room to drink the tea; Laura had little choice but to take her guest there, for there was only one rickety chair at the camping table in the kitchen. The room was refreshingly cool, but dark, so that she had to either open some shutters or turn on the lights.

'Please take a seat.' Laura retreated again to formal hostess mode, grateful for the 'vous' form of address to which they had both adhered throughout their conversation. Reluctantly, she turned to open the shutters. They clattered as she folded them back and the golden early-evening light streamed into the room. A breeze tugged at her hair, and she was suddenly conscious of her dishevelled appearance; it occurred to her that it was high time she had her hair professionally cut.

When she turned around, the priest was standing in the middle of the room, tea mug in hand, staring at the painting. For a while he said nothing. Captivated, his eyes wandered over the canvas, considering the old woman kneeling in prayer, facing the artist who looked down upon her from above. She was dressed in simple peasant blue against a dark background and the light fell on her bowed head, illuminating her wispy white hair in a halo of yellow. She had a red flower pinned to her chest, and in her hands she held red incense sticks, the smoke from which rose in swirls to heaven.

'Please do sit down,' Laura interrupted.

'I think I should not. I don't want to get paint on your sofa.'

'Please don't worry about that.'

At that, the priest seemed to give in. Suddenly weary, he slumped down, carefully cradling the steaming mug of tea in his hands, but he never took his eyes off the painting.

'It's a beautiful painting,' he said simply. 'I've never seen anything quite like it. Who is the artist?'

'It's by a Chinese painter, I doubt you will be familiar with him.' Laura hesitated, wondering whether she should add to her cover by saying that the painting was a copy, before deciding that the less said, the better. She beamed confidently.

'The artist fuses western and oriental influences and is best known for his portraits of peasant life.' Laura couldn't help herself. She enjoyed talking about art, and what would this country priest know about Chinese fine art, anyway? He was just making conversation. There was no danger that she might betray herself. They sat quietly together, sipping tea, eating peanuts, lost in the painting.

'My mother was a Catholic,' Laura said suddenly, loudly and boldly. 'A Chinese Catholic. She was tortured to death for her faith by Chairman Mao's Red Guards.' Her voice cracked, the words sticking in her throat, blood thumping in her ears. Why confess this now, to this man, in this place? It was a secret she had buried deep. No one knew about it, least of all her husband, and not even Little Swan. Having invited the priest into her home, was she now afraid of the intimacy? Did she want to shock him and hurt him so that he went away? Was it because it was all so unjust? Her mother had died for his Church, for his Jesus, and there had never been any redress. Ought he not to do something about it?

Putting down his cup on the coffee table, he looked her in the eyes, holding her in his gaze. Laura saw that he was struggling as much as she was.

'They put burning coals in her mouth to make her renounce her faith. But she would not.' She heard his sharp intake of breath, saw his jaw drop, a trembling horror spreading over his face. Lips pursed, she stared at him defiantly. 'That's why I don't believe in God.'

A few seconds passed, then Father Michael reached out and put his hand on hers. It was heavy and warm, streaked with paint, swollen with nettle stings. She let it rest there, staring at the halo of light around the old woman's head in the painting, feeling the pulse of him soothe her anger, hatred and grief.

'Laura, I wasn't always a priest. I was a soldier once,' he said, and began to weep. Great, silent tears tumbled. He made no attempt to wipe them away. And now it was her turn to sit there and hold his hand.

CHAPTER 13

What had happened to him during those two hours in the old house that had been shuttered on its own deadly secret for decades? He was a priest, no stranger to mystery, grief and pain. That was his job, and he never cried. Why had he broken down in front of a stranger?

It would not turn out well. All Father Michael's training and experience told him to keep his distance from Laura de Silva, the woman who did not believe in God but kept a picture of a peasant at prayer on her wall. It was no good getting close to single women in the parish, he knew that, and especially not this mysterious newcomer. There was something about her that he could neither explain nor understand; the way she had emerged from the sunlight and moved through the bushes, graceful, gliding, floating, conscious of the movement of every muscle in her body, totally in control. Despite himself, she wafted daily in and out of his mind. He thought of her when driving to a meeting, when washing up his coffee cup, at morning prayer; too often, she was there. He was vulnerable at the present time, doubting his role in the Church, even his faith. He was fully aware. Everything in his professional, rational, logical mind screamed at him. Stay away!

On Monday morning, Father Michael set out half an hour later than usual for his morning run, choosing a different route through the forest. It was already hot, and sweat streamed off him as he turned for the home stretch. It was then that he heard a familiar bark and saw Laura emerging from a path to his right. It occurred to him that she also had varied her route and timing.

'Bonjour, Father.'

'Bonjour, Madame.'

They might have passed each other in this awkward manner had it not been for the dog, who bounded up to Father Michael as if he were his long-lost friend. And so it was that the stranger and the priest walked on in silence in the shade, sheltered from prying eyes under the cooling canopy of trees.

Father Michael attempted practical chat. 'Have you thought of letting Boris off the leash and training him to come back?'

'I have, but the rescue centre people warned me not to. He's a street dog and might never return.'

They strolled towards the pale light at the top of the path. How softly she placed her feet! He felt gawky and lumpen at her side.

'Perhaps if you took Boris into the village a bit more so that he got to know people? That way, if he ran off again, you wouldn't be so worried. He certainly knew his way home last Saturday.'

'Perhaps you're right' Laura conceded. 'I think it.' Her vocabulary slipped. It surprised him, because usually each word was faultlessly placed, as if she were selecting it carefully from a box laid out in front of her.

Their path emerged from the trees at the top of the hill. Again, the two of them might have used it as an opportunity to move on, but the dog sat down, ears pricked up, smelling the air as if admiring the view. They were forced to stop, and stood for a while, enjoying the warmth of the sun on their faces and looking across the valley to the fields of sunflowers, a few of which were just starting to raise their faces. The view was half in shadow, the light still low and hazy. The scene reminded Father Michael of a section of their summer tapestry canvases, nearly a third finished, with the shadow of tracing paper sketched behind.

As local priest, he had not been convinced about the eight-hundredth anniversary commemorative tapestry initiative. So few of his parishioners ever showed up to Mass any more; in the days of cable TV and YouTube, it was impossible to compete. How could one expect people to show up regularly to sit and weave, of all things? Yet to his astonishment they had come, carrying their bottles of wine, baguettes, bowls of salad, boudin, ham, and cheese. Faithfully, taking shifts every Monday and Thursday night, they sat and wove. The tapestry was an heirloom, something for future generations, they said, and everyone wanted to leave a personal mark on it. Remarkable. Despite his initial misgivings, even he had got drawn in, and with practice his thick hands that had been trained on guns and hand grenades became quite deft with the cotton, linen and wool. All the while, as they worked, the tapestry teacher would tiptoe around the looms quiet as a mouse, whispering in people's ears.

'You're in the wrong profession, Madame Mini,' he had once told her. 'You ought to have been a priest.'

Following Father Michael's suggestion, Laura bent down and cautiously unclipped the dog's lead. He made no move to run away.

'So how did a soldier become a priest?' she asked quietly. The question was so gentle, so unexpected, but it had remarkable power. It caught him off guard.

'Ahhh, that is a long story.' Father Michael ran his hand through the fast-thinning hair on the top of his head. In that second it was as if a bomb, long dormant inside him, detonated. The forbidden words exploded out of his mouth before he knew what had happened.

'The truth is, I nearly murdered my best friend.' The priest lurched as if caught in the blast. Never in his life had he told anyone this, not straight out, not directly at least. He was more shocked by the confession than she was. But she did not flinch. She just stood there, calmly waiting. For him, at that moment, high on the hill, he was fixed in a trance, held fast by silence. Then, in the distance, he heard his voice, but he only half recognised it. It was his old voice, speaking the unutterable from long ago.

'I was an only child, an unruly one who could not be still. I preferred to be outside climbing trees, playing soldiers and making dens. As a teenager I hated school. The only thing I was good at was running. I would run for tens of kilometres, anywhere, around fields and streets. I would be gone for hours.' Again, he looked for her face, but it was hidden under the hat and glasses. It was as if not seeing her expression made him invisible, and that gave him courage to continue.

'My father was a politician and my mother a prominent socialite. Papa was a bully not just to the others in his party but also to me. I was terrified of him. I think my father saw me as an inconvenience, because my mother was very beautiful and he wanted her all to himself.'

Father Michael hesitated, reason and common sense reasserting themselves. What on earth had possessed him to surrender his secrets to Laura? Was it because he knew or sensed that she, just like him, was not who she said she was? But here his confession stalled, just short of the truth, the whole truth. There was hardly anyone left alive who knew his history; but in institutional memory, in police, regimental and secret service files, it would all be recorded. His father would have hated that: an open secret, giving the bureaucrats and his triumphant political opponents the last laugh, something to giggle and snigger about in corridors in the Élysée Palace, and over digestifs in the best Parisian restaurants. Of course, it mattered not a jot any more, but to his dying day his father had been a man who could not contemplate losing. Everything had been his son's fault, even the ultimate failure of his own corrupt political career.

The priest went on with the simpler version of his story. It was as if he were being propelled to go where he had feared to tread, that something had now started that could not be stopped. Whether that might turn out to be good or bad, he could not tell.

'I was and never could be good enough for my father. In the end I gave up trying. My mother died of cancer when I was eighteen, and he blamed me for that. After that I went to Paris to study law, but I was a lazy student, arrogant, self-centred and spoilt. Looking back, I wasn't a nice guy.' Father Michael swallowed and bent down to stroke the silky top of Boris's head.

'One day, when I had been drinking, I came home and found Beatrice, my girlfriend, in bed with my best friend. Seeing them together like that was a trigger for all my fury, resentment, frustration and anger. The dam broke. I'm ashamed to say that I beat Jean-Claude nearly to death. I would have succeeded if the concierge and my girlfriend had not pulled me off and brought me to my senses.' Keeping his eyes on the horizon and the sunflowers, Father Michael took a deep breath. 'If I'm honest, I was a coward. I took the Métro to the other side of Paris and presented myself at the gate of the barracks of the French Foreign Legion. The regiment gave me a new life, a new start. It was my family. In some ways, it perhaps still is.' Another uncensored sentence made him shuffle his trainers in the dirt. He did not tell her the rest: how his true identity had promptly been revealed when the Deuxième Bureau ran their usual security checks and discovered who his father was. Nor did he tell Laura that his father had intervened with the police to contain a national political scandal so that charges against him had never been pressed. The regiment had washed his identity and given him a new name, one that in a break with precedent, he had been allowed to keep, even after his discharge. Oh yes, and Jean-Claude had married Beatrice.

'That's quite a tale.' Laura smiled. She did not seem in the least shocked or surprised. She removed her hat, revealing a tangle of grey curls. 'And Victor, who will be coming for a holiday, is he a friend from the Legion?'

'Yes, he is', he replied, unsure how that information might be received. 'He's a good man. I would trust him with my life.'

'Excellent,' she said. 'But, Father, I'm afraid you did not answer my original question. You've told me how the boy became a man, not how the man became a priest.'

The dog stretched and stood up as if he too had been listening to their conversation. Deftly, Laura attached him back to his lead. 'Well done, Boris! You've passed your first test. Time to go home.' Abruptly, she turned to leave, walked half a dozen steps, stopped, then came back to the priest and removed her sunglasses so he could see her eyes.

'You know, it's bizarre. Once upon a time you were a soldier. Now you are a priest. I used to be a ballet dancer, years ago, in my past life.' Again she turned sharply away, as if her memories were as painful as his.

This time she made it to the edge of the clearing before pausing again and calling with false nonchalance over her shoulder. 'I was a member of a revolutionary dance troupe, trained in China'.

In the blink of an eye she was gone, her words left hanging in the still warm air so that Father Michael wondered if she had ever been there at all.

CHAPTER 14

The man was a giant. He filled the doorway of Laura's kitchen, and she would have been terrified if she had not been expecting him. Behind him was the priest, formal in dog collar and cassock, and Maddy wearing a voluminous red-and-white abstract-print linen dress.

'May I present Victor?' Father Michael said, and the giant offered Laura a huge, warm hand. He was wearing a T-shirt, and she noticed immediately the pink-and-white scarred skin that covered the backs of his hands and went all the way up his arms.

'A little present for you.' Maddy plonked a coffee machine and two packets of ground coffee on Laura's kitchen table. 'One always needs coffee!' Without waiting to be invited, she bustled about making a pot. A little overwhelmed by the size of Victor, Laura was grateful for Maddy's ice-breaking foresight. But if she were intimidated by the stranger, the huge man too looked tense and awkward, clinging on to his notebook and measuring stick like a boy on his first day at a new school. His face was dominated by thick bushy eyebrows and his black hair was peppered grey. He was dark for a Frenchman, with a curved nose that reminded Laura of the hook of an eagle's beak.

Father Michael began to explain the work that needed doing and, taking her cue from him, Laura produced the magazine cuttings she had collected to illustrate her ideas. She had rehearsed her words. 'Something very simple and classic, modern with a nod to traditional, in a bone cream colour, similar to the kitchen you fitted for Maddy.'

The kitchen filled with the aroma of freshly brewed coffee, and Maddy poured. She had even brought a couple of extra mugs with her. 'Victor likes his strong and black with two sugars.'

'At least three cups in a morning, preferably intravenously,' Father Michael joked, and reached up to pat his friend on the shoulder; Victor giggled, a strange squeak like something leaking air.

'And has Madame thought about the layout?' Victor spoke haltingly as if each word were an effort.

'Perhaps if I draw my ideas, then you can tell me what you think?' Laura pointed to the notebook in the man's hand.

How strange! He was different from most people, not least because he did not give her a second glance. It was as if he didn't notice her foreign face. He took his time examining her drawings and designs, sipping his coffee. He had large, sad brown eyes that were ringed purple with age, and several days' growth of stubble on his face. He was attentive to her ideas but did not smile again.

'Well, my friends, thank you for the coffee, but I am afraid I have to go. Duty calls,' the priest announced. Then, turning to Laura, he said, 'Maddy can help you to arrange things. Victor will get samples, draw up a plan and give you a formal quote. So, no need to worry.' He hesitated. 'See you later, Victor; you have your key?'

The huge man patted the back pocket of his jeans and gave a cheeky grin, revealing a line of perfect false teeth. 'Yes, Boss, not problem.'

Straight away he was eyes down, engrossed in the project; unfurling his measuring stick, meticulously measuring up, recording figures, diligently ruling sketches in his shiny new notebook.

***

It was nearly noon. Nothing moved in the summer heat. Laura stood in front of the bathroom mirror. That morning, she had taken the plunge and gone to the hairdresser's to have her hair cut short. It was now completely grey; she was truly the White-Haired Girl, the lead role in Madame Mao's revolutionary ballet of that name which, in her innocence, Laura had once so coveted. She could still dance it in her mind's eye, the scene where the evil landlord comes to the house, murders the heroine's father and drags her off to be his slave.

Life often mirrors fiction. Like the heroine she had danced all those years ago, Laura too had eventually escaped and was now hiding in the hills. But he would come for her, no evil landlord, but her husband and his henchman. It was only a matter of time. Tenderly she ran her fingers through her white curls and convinced herself for the first time in her life that they really were beautiful. Her face was deeply suntanned, and she had abandoned contact lenses in favour of a pair of simple black spectacles. Would he even recognise her now? With that question came a flicker of hope. Nonetheless, she adhered to a strict security routine, going online only when she needed to and always using her VPN. Once a month, at different times, shoulders tense, breath short, she would log in to her bank accounts, her company account in the Cayman Islands, and check her email. Only two people knew that address: the painter in Canada and her erstwhile broker in Rotterdam, who had died shortly after she fled to France. His son had taken over the business, but she'd had no further need of their services. Even so, it was only prudent to keep an eye out, just in case they tried to contact her. If either of them did, that would not bode well. Anxiously, Laura would rifle through her emails, including the spam, and sigh with relief when she found nothing from them.

Downstairs, water splattered into the metal sink in the utility room. It was the time when Victor was washing himself; his he did every day just before lunch. Through a half-open shutter, she watched him cross the garden and unroll his prayer mat under the shade of the apple trees, west to east, in exactly the same direction as the nave of the church. It had never occurred to Laura that the big man might be a Muslim. Every day she watched the quiet ritual unfold in the peace of the garden, but they never spoke about it; in fact, they rarely spoke at all. Laura understood from day one that, for whatever reason, small talk was painful for the man. He arrived about 8.30 a.m., his beard a little thicker every day until, now that the job was nearly done, it covered much of his face. She greeted him with a coffee and he responded with a smile. He spoke only when necessity demanded, to explain the progress of his work and consult when issues arose, all the while continuing to address her as Madame despite her requests that he call her Laura. He worked slowly but steadily, the heat forbidding any haste. She saw the pleasure he took in his work, how he stood back to admire the simplicity of a newly plastered wall, or the ordered, careful way he stacked the waste in the skip.

The lazy summer days sped by, and Laura relished each one. She knew she was resting in the eye of the storm. She got up early to take advantage of the cool, did her exercises, ate, and took Boris for his morning walk. She frequently ran into Father Michael and they would let the dog off the lead and walk and chat a while, careful to stick to innocuous topics: how to train Boris, the progress in her kitchen, the village tapestry. The rest of the day Laura would pass reading, shopping for food, exploring an antique sale or simply enjoying her garden. She bought an antique dresser for the bedroom, upon which she placed the porcelain doll and a blue-and-white washbasin. At least twice a week, she would walk to Madame Mini's barn on the other side of the village to sit and weave. She knew she was not universally accepted in the village, but that did not trouble her: the villagers did not know it, but this was safer for them.

Despite her fears and misgivings, Laura had allowed Maddy to put her on the weaving rota. Everything was all very well organised. Each of the four separate pieces of the tapestry was on a separate loom. Each loom had a number and a team assigned to it. Each team was responsible for delivering its completed section of tapestry by the end of the season. Weaving took place on Monday and Thursday nights from 7 to 8 p.m. There was then a half-hour shift change for food with a second shift working from 8.30 to 9.30 p.m. The barn was also open on Wednesday afternoons when school was out, and at other times by arrangement. Each team had its own meetings, lessons and targets, and each session was supervised by Madame

Mini. It was, Laura came to realise, an extremely serious, very bureaucratic and competitive enterprise, with each team vying with the others to produce the neatest work in the shortest time. Despite the competitive element, this was an environment she understood. It was not just the quiet time she spent at the loom; she revelled in Madame Mini's patient instructions, the joy of learning and chewing over the new weaving-related vocabulary that went with the camaraderie. In some bizarre way, this habit of coming together to produce something beautiful, reminded Laura of the ballet school. In the evening, tables had been set up in the yard outside the weaver's barn. The villagers brought wine and food and gathered there between shifts on the looms to eat and chat. Tired after a day's work, they would lean back in their chairs and grumble and moan, shadows falling over their faces as the evening wore on.

'So where are you from?' they would ask her; and, masked by falling night and with a glass of wine inside her, Laura found herself telling at least some of the truth.

'I was born in China. I'm a widow. After my husband died, I decided to move here. He was a businessman. Yes, I love this region. It's beautiful.' The more she repeated the tale, the more comfortable she became with it, so much so that she almost convinced herself. Perhaps they were all actors in a play and she was just an extra in the cast?

Laura watched the village characters come and go. Céline, who kept the register, would mark down absentees with a red biro in the right-hand column. Those who failed to turn up for their weaving session without explanation could expect a visit. Despite Céline's strict stance on attendance, she could down a bottle of wine in the blink of an eye and was the life and soul of the evening sessions. Madame Rossignol, always impeccably dressed, would sit at the head of the table, the queen to whom everyone deferred. God help anyone who sat in her chair by mistake! Then there was Sophie with her false eyelashes and gel nails: she worked at the estate agent's in Saumur, had just been dumped by her boyfriend and was utterly heartbroken. Confiding in Laura, she told her that working on the tapestry was 'excellent therapy'.

In the darkness, the villagers often seemed to forget that the foreigner was there. Not everything they said was understandable to Laura, but she enjoyed unpicking the sense of their chat and puzzling over the colloquialisms. Even when she lost the sense of their conversation, the music of their voices soothed and held her in its embrace. All the same, she found herself trying to discern the lines of power and influence. Old habits die hard. How could they possibly understand that where she came from, the Communist Party had eyes and ears everywhere? It was embedded at all levels of public and private life, in schools, neighbourhoods, businesses, even among family and friends. No one could be trusted, so people told others only what they needed to know.

Laura noticed that Madame Rossignol was only minimally polite to her. A tight-lipped nod and brief 'Bonsoir, Madame' was all she ever got. But it was plain to Laura that she was not the only one who was disfavoured. Madame Rossignol and the crotchety old Monsieur Santelli were not on speaking terms. Thankfully, one of these was on the later shift and the other on the early, but the atmosphere at change-over was sometimes tense. Every week, when the time came, Madame Mini or Maddy would tip off the old lady, who would nod and stand up from her loom and announce loudly to the assembled company in the most elegant and grammatically correct French,

'Alas, I regret that now I must leave.' With a dramatic wave, she would turn and make a sweeping exit via Madame Mini's house.

A few minutes later, Monsieur Santelli would hobble to the front of the yard, sucking on his pipe.

'Monsieur Santelli! I've told you a million times, put that bloody thing out,' Madame Mini would admonish him. If there was one rule that Madame Mini would not allow to be flouted, it was the smoking ban in the barn building. She was uncharacteristically fierce about it.

'My dear Madame Mini, you know I only do it to wind you up! Now, give me a kiss.' With that, he would proffer his bristly right cheek and make a grab for her waist.

'On your way, you old goat! Get in the barn and crack on with some work. No weaving, no wine and *no smoking*!'

CHAPTER 15

The months passed quickly. Father Michael and Laura stood at the top of the hill. Opposite them, the slowly browning sunflowers still stood bold and tall, heads turned towards the sun, proud like soldiers on parade.

'The kitchen will be finished by the end of the week.', Laura said. 'Victor says it will soon be time to shave his beard. I am thinking of holding a small party to thank him before he leaves. Just a few people, not more than six. What do you think?'

Father Michael thought for a while. 'If you invite people he knows, Maddy, Céline, Madame Mini, the Duguets, I think Victor would enjoy it.'

'And you too, Father. Will you come?'

He smiled. 'Of course.'

But Laura knew the priest's apparent pleasure was hiding something. He had been looking increasingly worn over recent weeks. She had picked up the scandal involving the bishop from the tapestry-weaving evenings and understood that the diocese was in turmoil. They stood for a while to listen to a skylark singing its heart out high above them.

'Father Michael, what happened to Victor?'

The priest sighed and waited for the skylark to finish singing before he replied.

'In the beginning, there were four of us. We joined the regiment at the same time, the Deuxième Régiment Étranger de Parachutists; crazy kids, each one of us with broken lives and nothing to lose. We were one Japanese, Osamu; one Algerian, Victor; one French Canadian, Luke; and me. Victor was the best solider among us, far and away the strongest, brightest and most determined. The four of us were inseparable, went through all our deployments and campaigns together; North Africa, the Gulf, Bosnia. Even when I was promoted to sergeant, it seemed to make no difference. There was no rancour between us. Truly we were brothers and the Legion was our homeland, just as our motto says.'

He paused and watched a tractor labouring its way up the hill from the distant river into the village.

'We all left the regiment after Sarajevo. To my amazement, I was accepted into theological college. Luke went to work as a builder in Tours. Victor and Osamu enrolled with a private security firm.' Father Michael let his eyes wander down to the village square, where he saw Duguet winding out the blue-and-white awning in front of the bar.

'It happened in Afghanistan. Osamu and Victor were escorting a group of foreign engineers when their convoy was attacked. The vehicle carrying Osamu took a direct hit from a rocket-propelled grenade. I will spare you the details, except to say that Victor pulled his friend's body out of the burning truck. He was never right after that. He didn't speak for months afterwards. He's had therapy and rehabilitation. The regiment looks after its own, but Victor has never really been able to cope with civilian life. It's difficult to explain and understand. He is a superb carpenter, which was his trade before he joined the regiment. He's happy as a fish in water fixing and making things, but just can't deal with the details of everyday life, things like putting in his washing, shopping, or preparing a simple meal.'

'He told me he lives at a retreat?'

Father Michael nodded. 'It's the regimental retirement home in Provence. They take care of his finances and accommodation and keep him busy. That way, he can keep his mind off things. He practises his religion discreetly and grows his beard when he comes here. It's sad. But it's just the way it is.' Father Michael reached down and scooped up a handful of soil from the path; it was parched from the summer heat. He rubbed it between his hands, then opened them and blew the bits of dust into the clear blue sky.

***

Laura's kitchen was finished. Madame Rossignol's kitchen sink was unblocked, Céline and Henri Duguet had a new electric shower in their bathroom, and Victor's summer holidays were over. He arrived for Laura's farewell lunch bearing a bunch of pink and yellow roses, obviously plucked from the presbytery garden. Clean-shaven, pepper-grey curls cropped flat to his head, he shyly announced that, as a Muslim, he was wearing his special rubber-soled shoes and would be happy to have his ration of wine. They were a small gathering; Laura, Father Michael, Maddy, Madame Mini and the Duguets, who had arranged cover for the bar for the afternoon. Laura had judged it best not to invite Madame Rossignol, although she felt it was an omission not to have done so, because Victor had also done work for her.

It was a beautiful day, and Laura had laid the large garden table under the shade of the trees. She had bought a large, blue-and-white chintz tablecloth from the market. It was in the Provençal style she had seen in her home design magazines, and she liked its fussy, old-fashioned femininity. Her husband would never have tolerated such retrograde rural design in the penthouse in Shanghai. Always hungry for the new, he demanded the latest gadgets, everything ultra-modern, smart, minimalist; marble, shiny black Italian leather. She was allowed nothing cosy to suggest comfort or home.

With Maddy's help to manage the new oven, Laura had roasted a chicken. This was a new experience for her. The kitchen in Shanghai had a western-style oven, but their maid never used it, and when Laura was small no one would have dreamed of owning such a device; food was prepared by frying or steaming over a gas stove. With an exaggerated sommelier's flourish, Duguet opened a bottle of Chablis and one of St. Emilion to accompany their meal. In addition to the chicken, Laura had prepared fresh lobster with ginger and spring onions, and a large plate of noodles. There was salad from the garden and baguettes from the boulangerie. It was late afternoon before they moved on to the cheese, which was followed by a dessert of fresh peaches and ice cream. Maddy had advised Laura that it wouldn't be a proper French luncheon without a cheese course, and Laura had obliged.

Leaning back in her chair, Laura surveyed her guests. Céline, head held high, chest puffed out to its limit, was doing a convincing impression of a peacock with the voice of Emmanuel Macron.

'Have mercy, Céline.' Father Michael said in mock protest at the sight of her bouncing bosom. Victor, who'd had more than his promised ration, wept with laughter.

The guests spoke quickly now, talking politics one minute and *Game of Thrones* the next, all without accommodating Laura, although she did not mind. They were all happy in the way that people in her own land had been when they came together to eat and drink at Chinese New Year. As they talked, a breeze shuffled the leaves of the trees above them and tugged at the flaps of tablecloth which Laura had pinned down with clothes pegs. Time was now slowed by the late-afternoon heat, the sunlight dappling the faces of her guests, everything lazy with alcohol and warmth. Laura felt as if she had walked into an Impressionist painting.

Suddenly, looped among the soft after-lunch chatter, Laura heard other voices: the deep gruff banter of men and a straggling snippet of song. It came like a whisper of breath, then disappeared. She poured herself a glass of water. Father Michael, whom Duguet had graciously invited to sit at the head of the table opposite the hostess, was telling a joke, his face chubby with wine and relaxation. A tuft of his thinning grey hair was caught in the breeze. It made Laura want to reach out and straighten it for him. He caught her eye and smiled as if to say thank you, and with a jolt Laura realised she was happy. It was an unfamiliar giggly, bubbling sensation that made her want to throw off her shoes and pirouette around the garden in the way she might have done once upon a time when dancing had been a joy.

Tipping back her head, she looked up at the sky but, in that instant, she felt her husband's hands around her neck. He had her on the bed in Shanghai, the full weight of his big body on top of her, his whisky-inflamed cheek pressed hard against hers. Tighter and tighter he squeezed, until she could not breathe.

'Whore! Think you can escape me?'

Looking quickly down, Laura forced herself to count the flowers on the tablecloth. It was an old trick she had sometimes used to calm herself, but it was too late. Here in this small French village, she understood that she now had something, something precious, to lose.

When the party was over, the guests helped to carry the crockery into the house and to tidy away the garden furniture. The men and Céline left with a flurry of kisses. Maddy and Madame Mini insisted on helping with the washing-up despite Laura's protestations that she now had a dishwasher. They were an efficient if eccentric-looking team, the diminutive, slight Madame Mini in her cheap white shirt and navy trousers contrasting with the bustling bottom and bulging arms of the expensively presented Maddy. They made short work of the task and then Maddy left, puffing out of the garden with Boris at her heels. Laura watched the dog go a little anxiously, but Father Michael's graduated exposure to dog training seemed to be having positive results. Boris would now walk to the top of the street and return home without problem. He had also twice accompanied Laura to tapestry weaving without incident, sitting contentedly between the looms and accepting strokes and titbits during supper.

The sun was all too soon dropping fast to the west of the church tower at the bottom of the garden, dragging the day with it to reveal a waxing moon. There was a welcome hint of coolness in the evening air. Madame Mini and Laura stood at the kitchen door watching the swallows swoop to catch insects, their wings making a soft whoosh with each pass.

'Before too long they will be gone, south to Africa for the winter.'

Laura was surprised. She was a city girl, born and bred. It had not occurred to her that the birds would migrate.

'Such a magical place you have here, a secret garden hidden from the world.' The tapestry teacher sighed, and Laura noticed how extraordinary the plain woman appeared in the gloaming. She was transformed. Her skin glowed and her brown eyes turned a sparkling amethyst. Perhaps she was a sprite or a fairy whose mysterious beauty was only revealed when the moon was rising? But that was the wine talking.

'Why doesn't Madame Rossignol like me?' Laura heard herself ask, and immediately regretted doing so. She sounded petulant, like a schoolgirl who had fallen out with a friend. She knew she was walking into a minefield, and would have preferred to make enquires in a subtler way. But Laura was tired. Again her customary caution and hard-won vocabulary had failed her, and she could not find the words to express herself adequately. This was the third time; the first had been with Maddy in her kitchen, and the second with Father Michael the day he had come for tea, and his fatal hesitation in response that betrayed all.

'Why did no one live in this house before me?'

Madame Mini rested her eyes on the glinting bronze lion perched on top of the church weathervane.

'They did. It belonged to an old family of the region. They lived here for generations, owned all the best vineyards.'

'That was before the war?'

Madame Mini paused. 'Do you have a cigarette?'

Laura returned to the kitchen and fished a packet and matches out of the kitchen drawer.

'I didn't know you smoked,' she said, opening the packet and offering it to the tapestry teacher.

'I don't!' Madame Mini chuckled, her eyes spitting purple.

'Neither do I,' said Laura.

'It's bad for you.'

'I know.'

The match flame sparked in the dark, releasing the timeless chemical smell that was like incense to Laura; it reminded her of her father lighting his cigarettes in their tiny apartment in Tianjin. Laura cupped the match for Madame Mini, then lit her own cigarette.

'Ah, c'est bien! It's been a long time.' Madame Mini inhaled deeply, holding the smoke in her lungs and puffing it slowly out of her mouth. The two women stood in silence a while as darkness fell. 'The burdens of the past weigh heavy on Madame Rossignol. She still grieves, even after all these years.'

The garden gate squeaked as Boris returned and padded across the misty patio into the house.

Madame Mini's face had dropped into shadow. 'This ridiculous pantomime between Old Santelli and Madame Rossignol, it has to stop. It has festered all these years,' she said, quietly. 'And you, Laura dear, are innocent. Look how you've given this house a new lease of life! It's a gift to us all.'

'Innocent!' Laura thought. That was the last thing she was. She had signed up for it. She had married him. In the beginning she had wanted the money, the modern lifestyle, as much as he did. After the years of eating bitterness, who could blame them if they felt they owed nothing to anyone, if they wanted to get rich quick? Everyone deserves a good life.

Madame Mini stubbed out her cigarette on the floor and picked up the butt to put in her pocket, but Laura reached out her hand to take it. How old was Madame Mini? She found it difficult to tell with westerners at the best of times, but with Madame Mini she was clueless. More than fifty, for sure, around her own age, perhaps? She seemed to have been born old and wise, and Laura treated her with the respect she might usually have reserved for someone much older.

'Enough is enough,' Madame Mini said, her eyes emitting shards of yellow. 'I will speak to Madame Rossignol. Please don't judge her harshly. Some say it is best to protect you from the past, but I think you need to know. I believe in fate. You came here to us in this village and this house for a reason, to break the wicked spell cast upon us a long time ago.' Repeating herself, she affirmed, 'It's high time we let bygones be bygones.'

'It's alright,' Laura whispered. 'I know about the ghosts. I hear them in the cellar and in the garden when the wind blows. They will not hurt me. I am not afraid.'

CHAPTER 16

Father Michael's heart thumped in his chest. Once again, he had tried to outrun the doubts that were gnawing at his soul. Some mornings this worked, but not that day. He was waiting in his running clothes in the clearing on the hill. Except he was not waiting, not deliberately waiting, that is, for the early-morning rendezvous between him and Laura were never quite fixed or arranged. They just happened. Some days he would wait for her. On others, she would wait for him, the dog coming on alone down the track in his direction to seek him out. On the rare occasions one or the other did not turn up, the next morning neither of them asked why.

He felt his heart rate slow and began to enjoy the nip of the early morning. The combine harvester had been out the day before, a great gulping, yellow machine, churning its way through the fields of sunflowers. The hill opposite had been stripped bare, leaving long naked strips of dark earth, and the bleak scene did nothing to lift the priest's mood.

Harrowing stories were continuing to emerge from the bishop's trial, and he felt betrayed not just by the man but by the institution. Hardly anyone was prepared to have their son or daughter confirmed any more, and it was difficult to escape the conclusion that the Catholic Church was a discredited and outdated institution. Was he a blinkered dinosaur, a servant to a glorious fantasy that perhaps had only ever existed in his imagination? Perhaps it was indeed time for him to resign his living, maybe even quit the priesthood. He knew he would not be alone if he chose to do so; other clergymen of his acquaintance had followed that route in a variety of circumstances. But who or what would he *be* without it, he wondered? Perhaps no more than a lonely and embittered old man? He tried to imagine life without celebrating Mass. The sacrament was the centre of his spiritual life, the foundation of his service. He knew many would not understand this in the increasingly secular western world, but he had always been aware of the joy in the simple ritual of breaking bread and sharing wine: it nourished, sustained and renewed all those who participated in the Mass. He had seen its power week after week at the altar rail throughout his priesthood. But the Church he served seemed incapable of meaningful reform and was responsible for terrible things.

Father Michael scratched his head. Night after night, his mind ran round and round the same track, faster and faster, into the early hours, knowing that unless he came to a decision sooner rather than later, he would go mad. He sought solace in the writings of St Francis of Assisi, which soothed with temporary relief like rubbing in a gently easing, time-tested balm. He had always understood that his faith was in some way independent of the Church, but the two had become so intertwined over the years that he now found it difficult to distinguish between them. If he dug out the root, could the vine thrive alone, or would it flounder and be squashed in the mud?

He stared south, where the mist lay in great swathes along the river valley. Resisting the temptation to look at his watch, he closed his eyes and listened to the silence. Of Laura there was still no sign. Perhaps this morning he would go away disappointed. Briefly, he wondered if she felt the same on the days when services or parish duties kept him away from the village.

In his moment of doubt, Laura arrived. He sensed her approach in the air, in the rustle of the trees, and then Boris loped out of the woods with a mischievous smile on his face.

'Hello, my friend. What's up?' Father Michael tickled the animal behind the ears, prompting Boris to utter a friendly low-pitched growl.

'He's getting fat!' Laura declared, eyes twinkling.

'Who's getting fat?' Father Michael teased her by putting his hand on his own midriff.

'Boris! The little devil has started visiting Madame Mini, the boulangerie, Madame Rossignol and heaven knows who else. I suspect they all give him a snack. I'm going to need to have words!'

Father Michael laughed. He loved the way she picked up French turns of phrase and delivered them with such aplomb. She clearly relished learning and improving her spoken French, as if it freed her somehow, though from what, he had no idea. When she got words right, her face relaxed, revealing a vivacious, intriguing woman. He wanted to reach out and lay his palm on her cheek, to hold her, to know everything about her, who she really was.

'I'm sorry,' 'he said, quietly, suddenly, without knowing why; the words seemed to be spoken of their own accord and were out before reason and rationale might check them. 'I'm sorry for what happened to your mother. It's a terrible, unimaginable thing.' He heard her sharp intake of breath, felt her stiffen at his side. He wanted to reach out and take her hand in his, but this time he dared not. Instead, they each rested in the early morning, taking pleasure in watching the birds scavenging over the fields below them.

'Thank you,' she said after a pause. 'No one has ever apologised, not the Party, not the Chinese State, not the Roman Catholic Church. It's as if it never happened.' She reached into her pocket as if looking for a cigarette, thought better of it perhaps, and removed her hand.

'For years I had little idea of what had happened to Mama. At the ballet school they told me she had died of pneumonia.' She patted her pocket once more, then inhaled deeply as if imagining the comfort of a smoke.

'I only found out because a former neighbour came to my father's cremation. There were only two of us there. She had been in the underground church with my mother and had been sent to the same labour camp for doing so. She told me that my mother was strong to the end and would not renounce her faith. She said I needed to know the truth of what happened.' Fists balled, seething with rage, Laura spat the woman's words. 'Truth! What truth? There *is* no truth. Sometimes I think it would have been better if she had never told me.'

Father Michael was at a loss. He tried to imagine the act of it, pushing burning coals into someone's mouth. Had this been enough in itself to kill her? Had she died of her wounds, of infection? But here his mind stalled with incomprehension and refused to consider matters further.

'What's your name?' Laura asked, abruptly changing the subject. 'Your real name, the name you had before the regiment?'

It took him a few seconds to catch up with her clever train of thought.

'Xavier.' The name emerged in a whisper, as if faded with neglect over the years. 'I was baptised Xavier François.' He omitted the famous surname. He could not bear to say it, and if he had, even she, a foreigner, would have been likely to work out who his father was, and he did not want that to happen.

'And your name, too, Laura, your real name?' he asked, gently.

She laughed – but kindly, as if he were a child who had asked a foolish question. 'Me! I have no name. I have been many things to different people. During the Cultural Revolution I had a ridiculous Communist name, all the children did at that time; 'Flower of the East.' She gave a comical, dismissive puff in the style of the village ladies. 'Then when I became a prima ballerina, they gave me another name, 'Fei Feng'. It means Flying Phoenix. But my mother and father'– her voice cracked with emotion – 'they used to call me Little Marrow, because I looked like a big fat one when I was all swaddled up as a baby.'

On the hill opposite, three large black crows arrived, circling with cackling caws, dive-bombing, chasing away the little birds.

'Last spring,' Father Michael began, 'not long after you arrived, I saw an angel. Do you think I am mad?'

Now it was her turn to be puzzled at a sudden twist in the conversation. 'Are we not all a little crazy?'

'The angel was a little girl with black hair and Chinese eyes. She was right here, and later she appeared to me in the church during Mass.'

For a long time, Laura said nothing, then ventured, 'And she was happy?'

'Yes. I think she was. When I first saw her, she was dancing in the fields below the hill.'

Another long pause ensued.

'I think your angel must have been my mother,' Laura said. 'She was born in Paris when my grandfather was a student there, studying engineering. They went back to China after he graduated, but I think Mama left her spirit in France. She used to talk about a house with a beautiful garden and a boat bed.'

'Is that what brought you here, Laura, to France?'

'It's a long story.' She wavered, looking him in the eyes, as if deciding whether to trust him.

She began cautiously, all the while testing his gaze. 'I grew up in the shadow of a great church: St Joseph's French Cathedral in the northern Chinese city of Tianjin. Have you heard of it?'

Father Michael shook his head.

'I loved standing among the washing on our tiny rusty iron balcony, admiring the three copper domes glistening in the sunshine, counting the different stones, a chequerboard of red and white. Such a beautiful church – I'll show you on the internet sometime. It looks somewhat like the Sacré Coeur in Paris, and it was built in the early 1900s, at the heart of what was then the French concession. Our apartment was on the street that led to the church, a wide boulevard lined with plane trees. One of our old neighbours had bound feet. I can see her now, hobbling up the street, resting at each tree. For years I thought that was what the plane trees were for: rest stops for the elderly and infirm. When I was young, the neighbourhood was very run-down and dilapidated, but even I could see that it must once have been very grand. People talked about the French as the stinking Imperialists, the foreign ghosts. As a little girl, I was terrified, imagining pot-bellied blue devils with horns and tridents, blood dripping from their mouths, hiding around every street corner, ready to jump out and gobble me up.' Laura laughed, but was instantly serious again. 'It wasn't until I was much older that I understood that the foreign devils were people who had lived in our neighbourhood and had built it in their own style. A few years ago, I visited the area again. It's booming now, in the new China. Would you believe that the whole street is lined with designer shops? How Parisian! Strange, isn't it, how lives return full circle?'

She broke off to look for Boris, who had run off into the bushes.

'Before he died, my father told me that after I was born, my mother would not rest until I was baptised. But Chinese Christians were persecuted by the Communist State. My dad was a Party member and a non-believer, but he was utterly devoted to my mother and kept her faith secret. In the end I think he was perhaps the greater believer. Finally, just before I was six months old, a priest came to our apartment, and the ceremony was carried out in secret.'

Laura frowned, concentrating hard, and Michael could see that she was struggling to find the words to express herself. He reached out and briefly touched her on the arm but pulled his hand back quickly, terrified by the strength of the contradictory emotions pressing upon his chest.

She continued. 'At that time, it would have been dangerous for my mother to bring me up openly as a Christian. Even an innocent child might say the wrong thing and unwittingly denounce their parents to the authorities. Although I did not find out the truth until years later, France was in my blood. At the ballet school, all the instructions were given in French; it's incredible, but even in Mao's China, French was the language of ballet. Most of my classmates found the alien tongue a battle, but it was second nature to me. It was then, as a trainee ballerina, that I began to dream, to remember my mother tucking me up in bed, singing to me, telling me stories, and praying. When I was a very small baby, she must have talked to me in French during the most intimate times of caring between mother and child. Snippets would come back to me over the years, often at night when I was alone and afraid. Our Father, who art in heaven…

'How was it that no one had ever taught me this prayer, and yet I knew it? And when I recited it in my head, I was safe again, in the big bed in our Tianjin apartment, with the smell of Baba's tobacco in the air and Mama's body soft and warm at my side. I never told anyone any of this, kept it out of the obligatory self-criticisms that the Party demanded. Young as I was I understood that if such knowledge were ever revealed, my career in ballet would be over. In later years, when life improved, I set about learning French. I suppose it was an escape for me. It allowed me to imagine a different world, to be someone and somewhere else.'

Laura stopped suddenly, as if afraid of what she had said.

But if Laura was afraid, so was Father Michael. He wanted to reach out, to put his arms around her, to hold her tight.

He was no stranger to women. There had been plenty when he was in the regiment. He had never paid for sex, and there was a time when he was proud that he could get by on good looks and charm. He had not lain with anyone since before Sarajevo, and although it would be na*i*ve to say that he had never felt the need to do so, this had never greatly troubled him. Where had these feelings come from now, after all these years?

He vowed not to meet Laura again tomorrow, to run along the road instead, although he hated that. He needed to get away. He would take a break before Advent at the house he had inherited from his grandmother on the Île de Ré. A bit of bracing Atlantic air would do him good, clear his mind. But he still did not make his excuses to leave and walk away. On the contrary, he asked for more.

'What happened to you, Laura, after they took your mother away? It must have been difficult.'

'Don't waste your sympathy on me,' she said, more sharply than she intended. 'I was a lucky one. People were starving, boiling tree bark to eat. At the ballet school, we were apparently in the vanguard of the Revolution, so we were privileged to have enough to eat.' Laura spoke quickly now, with more of an accent, jumbling up her vocabulary, making uncharacteristic grammatical mistakes, slipping sometimes into English, sometimes into Mandarin, so that he had to help her find the right words. None of this confession was rehearsed.

'I remember the last spring when we were together as a family. Schools were closed and Red Guards were on the streets. I was a child, but I witnessed it all. They dragged the priest out of the church, hung a wooden placard around his neck, denounced him in front of a baying crowd and beat him. My parents stopped talking to the neighbours. People scuttled about, hunched up as if trying to make themselves invisible. My mother was always looking over her shoulder. She hardly spoke to anyone, and if she did, it was not more than a few hasty words exchanged in passing on the corner of a street. Often my whole body would tingle and blood would rush to my head. Everything was surreal. I felt as if everyone I knew was acting, pretending, playing some sort of game I couldn't understand. Why couldn't the grown-ups see how ridiculous they all were, peppering their conversations with tributes to the Great Helmsman and the Communist Party, spouting gobbledygook from some Little Red Book? But, I calculated, if the adults were taking it all seriously, then it must be true. Probably I was too young to ever understand and was missing something important.'

Laura made her back ramrod-straight, composed her face, and declared the words once required of her. 'Revisionism, or Right opportunism, is a bourgeois trend of thought that is even more dangerous than dogmatism. The revisionists, the Right opportunists, pay lip service to Marxism; they too attack dogmatism. However, what they are really attacking is the quintessence of Marxism' At the sudden realisation of the absurdity of this dogma, she burst out laughing.

This allowed him to do the same. 'I'll tell you a secret, Laura. As a little boy, I remember sitting in church one Easter and hearing the story of Lord Jesus rising from the dead. I thought it too incredible to be true. But look at me now!'

'You had doubts even then?'

'Of course. I still do.'

He saw a flicker of shock and surprise on Laura's face, but she passed no comment, and he was grateful for that.

They stood for a while looking at the village below, the little children like ants, trailing with their mothers along the road to school.

'It's a strange thing', Laura continued. He could see that now she had started to talk, she wanted to finish. 'Despite the chaos and insanity all around us, those last months at home with my parents were a happy time. They were incredibly gentle and kind to me. My mother would brush my hair until it shone, and she would let me wear it loose around my shoulders in bed. They gave me the tastiest bits of food from their own plates and cuddled me to sleep every night. But I found this bewildering, because I wondered what I had done to deserve such love. Looking back now, I can see they were giving me all they could before it was too late, preparing for what was to come. But how can you give a lifetime of love in a few days?' Laura's voice cracked.

'Shall we sit down?' Father Michael said, and priest and ballet dancer sat together on the narrow bench at the back of the clearing.

'Like you, Xavier, I was a very physical child. I loved gymnastics, was always hanging myself upside down and standing on my hands. My happiest memories are winter ones, of when my parents took me to the frozen lake to skate. My father was a superb amateur skater, skilled at jumping, spinning and racing. I had no idea what freedom meant back then, but veiled by the early-morning mist out on the lake with him, I knew we possessed something special. There, everything was different, sound, space, even the passage of time. There were no walls, no neighbourhood watch, and we were free to be whatever we wanted. We glided like swans, describing great arcs in the sky with our hands and arms. We flew like dragons, and carved flowers and suns on the virgin ice using the blades of our skates. Those winter days when the lake froze over were always too few and too short.'

Laura sighed, stretched out her arms, and lifted her head to the rising sun. 'I used to think it was my talent for skating that led me to ballet. My parents knew about Madame Mao's prestigious revolutionary ballet troupe and took me for an audition. I remember it vividly; hundreds of children in a freezing cold hall. A tiny woman, whom I later came to know as Teacher Wang, made us stretch, bend and tumble, pushing our little bodies this way and that. She seemed to be particularly unforgiving with me, pulling my left leg right up to my shoulder to test my flexibility. My instinct was to cry with pain, but something told me that what I was trying to do was important to my parents, so I gritted my teeth and did not complain. The miracle was that I was given a place at the school when everything about my petit-bourgeois class background was wrong. It wasn't until years later that I understood the full truth about a deception and conspiracy that had a terrible price for me and Teacher Wang.'

She dropped her head, looking at her hands folded demurely in her lap. In the trees, a single dark-coloured bird began to sing cheerfully to wake up the day. 'My parents knew that it would not be long before the Red Guards came for them. People in the neighbourhood were aware that my mother had grown up in France and had been a Catholic, but that was only the half of it. Thank God they did not know the whole truth about us. In those days, a mere whiff of foreign association was enough to condemn. Looking back, it was amazing that we lived undisturbed for so long. I can only suppose that my father must have used his influence in the Party to protect my mother. By sending me to the ballet school, my parents were trying to keep me safe, to give me a future in the world as they saw it at the time.

'The school was in a distant city, so I had to board the whole year. It was a brutal regime with long hours of training and, of course, political studies. I cried myself to sleep every night for months, everyone did, even the tough country children. But I was able to find some refuge in the clunking music of the old piano, the movement and the dance. I was thin, light and flexible, quick to learn, with big eyes, a small mouth and pale skin and a good sense of rhythm. For better or for worse, that marked me out.'

Laura looked up. The sun was beginning to penetrate the clouds, lifting the mists over the river.

'At the end of my first year, I had achieved good grades and was so excited about going home for the summer when the Director called me into his office. Teacher Wang was standing straight and tall by his side. People said she had been a much-favoured ballerina and a great beauty, but with her hair cropped short and the thick lenses of her glasses, I could not imagine it. She was the wickedest of teachers, and she had it in for me. It was not until I became a prima ballerina that I found out why.

'The Director said nothing, just looked me up and down. I was too young to fully understand, but I knew it was wrong. It was Teacher Wang who delivered the news, straight to the point'. 'It is my duty to tell you that your mother has died and your father has gone to serve the Party in Tibet.' She added that I had worrying bourgeois tendencies and instructed me to write a self-criticism, as if my mother's death were my fault. If, and only if, the Director were satisfied with my essay, would I be allowed to stay in the school because of my dancing ability.

'I was stunned, so much so that I could not grasp the idea that my mother was dead. I was also worried about my self-criticism. I knew it had to meet with the Director's approval, but I couldn't think what to write. In the end, I confessed to taking an extra steamed bread bun at breakfast the previous week when the cook wasn't looking. Believe it or not, that was a lie!'

The dam had been broken now, and Laura talked even more quickly, as if she wanted to get it over with. 'When I was sixteen, I got the lead role in a ballet, *The White-Haired Girl*. I was over the moon, for I had achieved my goal. It meant that I was as good as the best female dancer in the company, Little Swan. It was then that the Director claimed his prize. My virginity, for his silence on the matter of what he called my "little class secret".' There was no emotion in Laura's voice now; she spoke clinically, precisely again, in a way that forbade sympathy.

'Teacher Wang came to pick me up in a big black car with dusty beige curtains on the windows. A car! They were only for senior Party officials. Nothing in my upbringing had prepared me for what happened in the hotel with the Director that night. Afterwards I cried, and Teacher Wang slapped me viciously, once on each cheek. "Selfish girl. Do you ever think about me? Do you?" She shook me so hard that I bit my tongue and spat out some blood. 'Grow up, girl! Stop whining. This is the price we all have to pay to survive. Do you think you are the only one this has ever happened to? You're not the first and you won't be the last. And what about the sacrifice I have made for you?" I had no idea what she was talking about, but eventually she told me.'

'I learnt that she had grown up with my mother in Paris. When they were little girls, they had been best friends – and she was actually my godmother! What she had done had carried great personal risk. Nonetheless, she had agreed to become my godmother out of love for my mother. She asked me: how did I think with my background I had been offered a place at the ballet school in the first place? Where did I think my curls, my pale complexion and my long slim legs had come from? It was high time I knew the truth and the whole truth. Then she told me that my father, the man whom I called Baba, was not my real father. It was as if she had hit me again, harder this time, in the stomach. But she went on calmly, demurely, enjoying my distress. She told me that when my mother was young, she had worked as an interpreter in the diplomatic compound in Beijing. While there, she'd had an affair with a French diplomat, a Monsieur de Rouvoy, and became pregnant with me.'

In that instant, Father Michael saw the quiet presence in the squareness of Laura's jaw, in her earnest brown eyes with subtle double eye-lids, and the tumble of thick grey curls; perhaps the shadow of the diplomat who had been her father. He had a vision of the man, a minor aristocrat, perhaps, with a name like that, who thought the world owed him a living. The priest had come across enough such folk in his time; for a brief period in his own life, he had even been such a man himself. His own father had been very proud of their family pedigree. But Father Michael understood that Laura's origin was what had defined her beauty and made her stand out. He yearned to put his arm around her, to make everything right, to keep her safe, but he knew that if he did that, there would be no turning back for him.

Laura continued to tell her story, pragmatically and less emotionally now, simply stating the facts as she had learnt them. 'It seems de Rouvoy was married, and when my mother told him she was going to have his baby, he left Beijing overnight, taking his family with him. My mother never heard from him again.'

At this point, Boris emerged out of the bushes and trotted over to his mistress, tail wagging. Pulling him to her, Laura hid her face in his neck, nuzzling him, whispering sweet nothings in Mandarin. Around them and Father Michael, high in the trees, other birds began to sing. At length, Laura sat up. He saw that her eyes were red with tears.

'Years after my mother's death, I found out that Baba, the man who brought me up as his own daughter, had been denounced as a Rightist. Grief and years in labour camps broke him, body and mind. By the time I saw him again, I was the adult and he the child.'

At last, Father Michael did reach out and put his arm around Laura's shoulders. She did not soften to him, nor did she pull away.

'I am sorry,' she said. 'I should not have burdened you with all this.'

The last strands of mist were lifting, and the Loire glinted a promising blue in the golden light. Cautiously, she reached out her hand and laid it on his. It was a delicate hand with long thin fingers, roughened a little by gardening. There was no pressure in her touch, yet as she talked it weighed heavier and heavier, and he felt the pulse of her entering him.

'You are lucky,' she said quietly. 'You believe in God.'

'Most of the time. I have my moments.' When she spoke she used 'tu', rather than the formal form of address, and Father Michael felt barriers collapsing inside himself. He could no longer pretend. Here outside the village with Laura, high on the hill, he was not a priest but a man.

'I believed in God once, for a short time; we all did.' Laura said. 'As Madame Mao's famous revolutionary dancers, we were fervent followers of the Chairman. They brought us up to be that way. We worshipped and adored Mao. God forgive me, I even fantasised about dancing for him. There was a time when I would have laid down my life for him, like my mother did for Jesus… No, really! Don't laugh! After Mao died, we were hollow inside. We had dedicated our lives to the Party and Chairman Mao. Without him, what was there to live for? Our whole world fell apart.' Laura clapped her hands, the single sound echoing like a gun-shot across the valley, scattering the birds from the surrounding trees. 'That's why I don't believe in anything any more, just this.' She gestured to the sleepy village laid out like a toy model below; to the sunshine, the ribbon of river, the sky and the trees. 'The here and now, the moment. For me, that's all there is.'

CHAPTER 17

Bill Winston checked his rear-view mirror. The road was clear for miles behind and disappeared arrow-straight over the distant horizon. He put his foot down on the accelerator, smashing the speed limit. Gone was the jovial ice cream seller, replaced by a ruthless man determined to get what he wanted. He did not have much time left. Every second counted.

Two weeks ago, he and Vivien had closed their ice cream shop for the season and he had gone to help settle his wife back in Vancouver. She would spend the winter there, playing mah-jong, nattering and eating dim sum with her friends. But Bill could not escape the city fast enough. For him, living there felt like drowning. The large number of Chinese in Vancouver reminded him too readily of something he had left behind when he emigrated.

The past year had been particularly unsettling. Latent tensions, many dating back generations, were now there for all to see, especially in some of the larger restaurants where the lines between contending factions were drawn between neat white restaurant tables. Similar divisions were palpable in hairdressers' and dentists' chairs, basketball courts, classroom desks, pharmacists' counters, clothing-store changing rooms and beauty salons. Some neighbours chose to no longer acknowledge each other, and even shopping malls could be distinguished by their clientele. The previous week, when Bill and Vivien had presented themselves at their usual restaurant, popular with one faction, they had been ignored and passed over in the queue. One diner had even sneered, 'Big Six mainlanders! We don't want you here,' using a derogatory term directed at those who came from mainland China and did not therefore speak Cantonese.

'We are Canadian, just like you,' Bill had replied, feeling his temper rising.

'Leave it! We can go somewhere else.' Vivien was always the cool head, the one with common sense.

'Fuck them!' he had said loudly as she steered him away.

Despite himself, he knew that retreat had been the wiser option. He was only too well aware that many of the political, ethnic and linguistic issues in a country thousands of miles from Vancouver were being played out on the streets of the Canadian city. An associate of Fei Feng's husband had 'been disappeared'. Such events added to Bill's anxiety, and he wondered whether his past would not catch up with him. Although he had been lucky so far, he made himself check his Hotmail account to see whether Fei Feng had been in touch.

There had been nothing for a long time. He thought it more than likely that she, like him, judged that silence was the safer option. This conclusion pained him because, in his own way, he had loved her very much. Fei Feng, the beautiful ballet dancer, had been kind to him, but he was never foolish enough to hope that she could ever feel for him as he did for her. If anyone had asked him about the picture of her that he'd painted the first winter he spent alone in the cabin, he would have said that she was his first, last and only muse. But he was well aware that without Fei Feng's business acumen, imagination, contacts and cunning, he and his family would never have been able to emigrate to Canada. Their daughter, Melissa, could never have experienced the freedom and opportunities that she now enjoyed.

At the thought of his daughter, his heart skipped a beat. She was his pride and joy, although in some ways he hardly recognised her these days. She was studying medicine at the University of Alberta and had become a talented figure skater. Gone was the shy, slight girl who had come with them from Shanghai. She had grown into a tall, voluptuous, super fit, confident Canadian with a perfect and expensive gleaming smile.

The roads in the province of Alberta were much wider and easier to navigate than those in British Columbia, and once he had crossed the state boundary, progress was quicker. The dashboard GPS indicated two hundred miles to his next turning. If Bill Winston carried on breaking the law at this speed, he could be at the cabin for the golden hour around dusk and go down to the river to take some photographs.

Leaning back in his seat and taking a slug of cold coffee from a plastic cup, he glanced at the mountains. He was eager to get painting, his mind firing, overfilling itself with ideas. Every painting season was a fresh adventure, and when he painted, he was excited, terrified, exhilarated and anxious, all at the same time. His art was, as his wife understood, a compulsion, an addiction that he could not live without. She had often said it would be the death of him if he had to stop painting. Bill put his coffee cup in its holder and tapped his fingers on the top of the steering wheel. His wife was a good woman, but he failed to understand why she could not embrace the majesty of the wilderness. He couldn't get enough of the Rocky Mountains: the endlessness, the scale, the glory, the wonder. She, on the other hand, was terrified of the great expanse of Canadian space. It seemed to shrink her. While he chose the mountains, she opted for shopping malls. 'Living in the real world', she called it, but he thought the city the greater illusion. In the end they had reached this compromise. He would next return to Vancouver for Christmas to spend time with her and Melissa. After that, weather permitting, he would squeeze in a few more weeks in the wild before the Chinese New Year. He did not want to miss winter in the cabin. During the dark, lonely, painful nights, he produced some of his best work.

'At last!' Bill stepped out of the car, stretched, and breathed in the fresh mountain air. Already his eyes were expertly scanning the horizon in the direction of the Athabasca River. He did not have much time before the light would go completely. He fired up the generator and checked the gas levels in the cabin before unloading his food provisions from the truck. He put the frozen goods into the top of the refrigerator and took the crates of oranges to the outhouse. Everything else he left until later. He had escaped to the cabin for twenty-four hours several times over the summer to do maintenance and chop wood. All was ready for his return.

Grabbing his camera, jacket and hat, he set out on the trail behind the cabin. Bill's cabin was the penultimate of seven set into the hillside of a narrow canyon. There was a small hotel at the bottom which ran dog sled tours in the winter. The location was known mostly only to the locals, and thus mercifully off the main tourist trail. Originally, Bill had wanted to purchase the cabin higher up because the views from the porch were better, but the building lay just outside the signal range for cell phones. Once again, a compromise had been reached between husband and wife which showed that Vivien had been right. He had to be able to get in touch with his family and would have been miserable if he had to miss out on his weekly Sunday afternoon chats with Melissa. Hearing his daughter's confident laugh, listening to her recount her adventures, was a joy. She spoke to him in a Shanghainese dialect with a bizarre rising Canadian intonation that made every sentence she uttered sound like a question. But he loved her for it. Not wanting to disturb the silence, Bill trod softly. He stopped to rest his hand for a few seconds on the trunk of a great pine tree, trying to hear the pulse of the earth.

'Hello there!' he said to the world around him. 'I've missed you.'

The trail climbed steeply for a while, and Bill began to pant. After the ice cream season, he was less fit than he needed to be. This was always remedied by time spent at the cabin in the winter, as Vivien had once reluctantly conceded, poking him sharply but affectionately in the belly; he lost weight and became fit. At the top of the hill, he turned sharply left and descended steeply. A short distance later, he emerged on the shoulder of a broad creek which eventually fed into the Athabasca River. He stopped and gasped for joy, knowing that he was indeed blessed.

There it all was: had he found it, or had it been waiting for him, preparing for this moment all summer long? On the near bank, the tiny maples flamed rust-red, while the deciduous trees were turning gold. Beyond the far bank, the mountains rose sharply in the distance, austere black and white, the peaks and middle slopes already thinly covered with snow. Between the banks ran the creek, separating the winter from the fall, the whole scene tied together with a crystal-blue sky flecked with pink. Bill stared, drinking in the slowly changing colours, translating the scene in his mind ready for a canvas. Cautiously, he took out his camera, fearing that the simple act of doing so might chase the moment away. Turning this way and that, he took the first dozen shots, then sat down to wait.

It was impossible at this stage to tell when the light would be at its best for him to try to capture it in a painting. Sometimes he thought he had captured the moment, but then the climax came a minute or two later. It had taken him years to perfect his style and techniques for painting the mountains. He did not want insipid, rustic scenes in the style of the Swiss Alps. At the end of his first winter in the cabin, he'd sold a painting to a tourist: misty mountain peaks, with a tiny light in a cabin set in the bottom right-hand corner. He was ashamed now to think of this piece as what it undoubtedly was: a piece of kitsch. The rest of his canvases from that first season he had thrown on the fire, disappointed with himself for not producing the better work of which he knew was capable. Eventually, after years of trial and error, he had the courage to abandon the constraints that had been imposed on him in art school and by the forgeries he had provided for Fei Feng. At last, he had found himself and begun to paint in an abstract, free form with a focus on colour and shape. This had enabled him to produce vivid landscapes full of the contrasts and colours that had become his trademark.

But now, as he stood by the creek, the wind was getting up, sending wisps of white clouds scudding across the sky and dragging a dark purple in their wake. The water also began to ink over, and the trees retreated into shadow. Bill blew on his fingers, snapped a few more pictures and, shivering, turned for home.

The cabin was small, with just one bedroom, a shower room and a kitchen-cum-living space. It was sparsely furnished, the main room dominated by Bill's easel and work table. When he ate, he sat either at the kitchen bar or on the old leather settee.

Growing up in Mao's Shanghai, as one of four children, there had been no such thing as privacy. The closest he had got to it was when using the outside privy. Even then, there had always been people banging on the door.

'Hurry the **** up! I'm bursting!'

After he had married, the government had allocated him and Vivien an apartment. It had seemed like a palace at the time, but after Melissa was born and he had started to paint to earn a living, the stress of three of them living and working in two rooms had taken its toll on their marriage. For Bill, privacy, peace and solitude were the ultimate luxuries.

He lounged on the settee in the cabin, cradling a glass of Japanese malt whisky, which he much preferred to Scotch or the Irish brands. Putting his feet up on the coffee table next to his emptied noodle bowl, he tipped back his head and sighed. Alone in the cabin, with a full belly and the flames roaring in the stove, Bill Winston was a rich man. In front of him on the main wall, where others might have expected a television to be, he had hung his portrait of Fei Feng. Sipping his whisky, his eyes idled over it, caressing her naked shoulders, feeling her skin warm, soft, porcelain-white, her eyes wide and black as night, begging. He tasted her sweet cherry lips, flying with her, losing himself in the long black mane of curls blowing wild and free in the breeze. He raised his glass to Fei Feng, the mysterious ballerina he had possessed so many times in so many ways, but never more than in his dreams. Wherever she was in the world, did she ever think of him now? Was she even still alive? Had those who wished her ill, or perhaps even dead, found her wherever she now was? He shuddered, quickly downed the rest of the whiskey in his glass, and poured himself another double.

CHAPTER 18

Laura stood in her pyjamas at the open bedroom window, looking up at the moon. It hung full and low to the right of the church steeple. Reaching out, she covered it with her hand, then pulled it back to her, as if catching a dandelion puff. There would be a Festival back home. The streets of Shanghai, garlanded with lanterns, would be thronging with families, the children wide-eyed with excitement, woolly hats pulled down over their foreheads, prudently wrapped in winter jackets against the evening chill.

With a neat swerve practised to perfection over the decades, Laura indulged no more in thoughts of children. She preferred to think of Little Swan and the other dancers who once, before she met her husband, had been her friends. They were young again, laughing around the dinner table, chopsticks working double time, talking with mouths full, pulling legs, playing the fool, and making jokes. Afterwards, they would light lanterns and eat moon cakes; looking up at the moon, they would dare to dream.

The last thing Laura had expected in France was to feel homesick, but the cruel longing had come with a vengeance. At night, wrapped in her winter duvet, she had roamed the streets and alleys of Shanghai, looking up at the lines of washing hung from balconies, dreaming of food and the smell from dozens of sizzling-hot woks. She came to know which stalls and restaurants served the best delicacies. Often in her dreams, she found herself eating little dragon dumplings at the street stall round the corner from Bill's flat. She was wearing Gucci shoes and he plastic flip-flops, both of them burning their mouths in their eagerness to taste the dumplings' juicy, meaty filling, then laughing at their foolishness. Those had been the innocent days, when neither of them confronted the criminal nature of what they were engaged in. She sometimes blamed herself for dragging the shy, quiet man into their enterprise, but he could have left at any time and she would not have held it against him. They had always been honest and fair in their dealings with each other. She had promptly paid him half of the proceeds of any sale, and she never led him on, although she was well aware that he adored her. When it had come to the final multi-million dollar deal, they had discussed it and he had readily agreed to it and with his eyes open.

Nonetheless, every night here in the village, Laura dreamed of the tastes of home, sweet heightened by sour. Every morning, she awoke wanting food, but she knew this appetite could not be satisfied with food alone. It was the curse of an exile, part of her soul always hankering after the place where she was born and had grown up. Perhaps the curse could be mitigated or even lifted by preparing some of the meals she had enjoyed in the country of her birth, but to do that required a range of ingredients that could only be found in a Chinese supermarket. Laura knew that there was such a supermarket in Tours, but going there was not without risk. Nonetheless, she judged it a risk she had to take.

It was barely 10.30 in the morning when Laura arrived at the small shop in an immigrant suburb of the city. It was a basic place with neon strip lighting and a concrete floor, and she was the only customer. In the back of the shop and in awkward spaces, boxes of goods were stacked, waiting for their contents to be put on the shelves. Freezers and chilled cabinets buzzed loudly. As she stood in front of them, Laura eagerly examined what was inside. Her instinct was to grab a little of everything and get out of the place as quickly as she could. Fortunately, wiser counsel prevailed, as she realised that a hasty, seemingly random large purchase would serve to draw an unwelcome attention to herself. She glanced up at the large security mirror in the back left-hand corner of the shop and the security camera in the other. Forcing nonchalance while she carefully checked the eat-by dates, she chose a couple of packets of tofu – one soft, one smoked – some frozen prawn dumplings, and sweet soup rice balls. Sesame was her favourite flavour; it had been Little Swan's, too. When her friend was dying, Laura had made a broth of sweet ginger, added the rice balls, and taken the soup in a thermos flask to the hospital. It had been the last meal they would eat together.

Today, Laura calmly picked up two packets and a third with red bean filling for good luck. They kept well in the freezer, so would not waste. She next raided the dry food section of the store, walking slowly down an aisle and selecting a wide range of familiar foods. She pleased at how easily she read the Chinese characters on the various packets. Her homeland now seemed very near, and this terrified her, prompting panic to rise in her chest. She felt as if the walls of the shop were collapsing in on her. She swallowed hard and for a few moments struggled to breathe. It was then that she realised how far she had come: the months in France had transformed her. She was a different person, and she could never go back, even if she wanted to.

Two women stood wrapped in cheap winter jackets at the check-out, their hands in fingerless gloves. It was freezing in the shop. Perhaps the owner was too tight to heat it. Their faces were pinched with poverty and the evident harshness of their lives. They might have been transported from a rural Chinese village just the previous day. The younger woman, clearly the daughter, wore make-up that did nothing to soften her appearance; on the contrary, the attempt at beauty made her appear even more rough and tough.

Laura judged a breezy French courtesy to be the best option. 'Bonjour, Madame.'

'Want a bag?' the red-faced older woman grunted in heavily accented French.

'No, thank you. I have one.' Laura continued with her strategy of light politesse.

Slowly, as if it were a great effort, the mother began to lift Laura's goods out of her basket. She ran them over the scanner sullenly, and then plonked them down for Laura to pack. Laura bit her tongue. She wanted to tell the woman to hurry up and not be so rude. Instead, she distracted herself by looking around at the array of hand-written adverts pinned to a large board behind the check-out. A glance told her the board had all the expected sorts of notices, prominent among which were those with tear-off slips giving mobile numbers for vacant rooms and flats to let. There were also rows of SIM cards, their bright packaging making them impossible to ignore.

Looking around, Laura spotted two grainy black-and-white CCTV screens behind the till. All this time, the younger woman had never looked at her sole customer, but had been watching these screens. Laura saw herself in the larger one, dressed in a plain black jacket, her beautiful heart-shaped face clearly framed by her white woollen hat. Seeing herself on the screen, she regretted allowing the cloudy day to lead her to decide not to bring her dark sunglasses.

***

Later that afternoon, Madame Rossignol opened the big blue gate to let herself into Laura's garden, and, by chance, Laura caught sight of her from the bedroom window. Dressed in a navy raincoat elegantly pinched in at the waist, she wore a cream cloche and matching scarf, and carried a red wicker trug on her arm. Her attire was of a completely traditional style and it could have been lifted off a fashion plate. Laura noted that Madame Rossignol had come out without her stick, suggesting that she was much fitter and more agile than she perhaps led others to believe.

Her visitor crossed the gravel drive and the garden as if she owned the place. She stood, shading her eyes, their gaze taking in the trees rustling in the breeze, the expanse of the well-cut lawn, and the church tower that stood out against the backdrop of washed-out grey clouds that threatened rain. Slowly, Madame Rossignol wandered to the end of the garden, surveying all as she went and nodding her head as if talking to herself. Thinking that perhaps the old lady was unwell, Laura went downstairs and out of the front door. By the time she arrived at the doorstep, Madame Rossignol was near the house, examining the roses. Only a few were left. One by one she lifted their drooping heads, still damp with morning rain, savouring what was left of the scent.

'I'm afraid the roses are nearly finished,' Laura said quietly, so as not to startle her visitor.

But it was as if Madame Rossignol knew Laura was there. 'I can't believe the roses are still here after all these years.'

'They had gone wild, but I thought they were so beautiful, I had not the heart to pull them all out.'

'Autumn is the time when you need to prune them back – severely but carefully.' She bent to show Laura, placing her gnarled, wrinkled index finger across the stem as if it were a knife. 'Be ruthless with them. That way they might flower well again next year.'

'Thank you. I'll do that. Would you like come in and have a cup of tea or coffee?'

But it was as if Madame Rossignol did not hear the invitation.

'When I was a child, I used to play here. There were four of us, thick as thieves we were: Bernard, my brother; Jean-Louis, the youngest son of the Blanchard family who lived here; Guy Santelli; and me. Yes, once upon a time, that grumpy old stick Santelli and I were friends! It's hard to believe now, I know. Look! See where the branches splay on that beech? That was our airship. We flew all around the world and had many adventures in that!'

'You climbed all the way up there?'

'We did.' The old lady smiled proudly and looked at Laura as if for the first time. Then her face hardened, she squared her shoulders and she turned to face the house. 'We had many happy times here, before the war. The only thing I did not like about this place was old man Blanchard. Such a coarse man, with a loud voice and steel-grey eyes. Even the boys were wary of him, for he had a fast fist for cuffing around the ear. I have never been back to this house, not until today.'

'Please, you must come in and sit a while.' Laura renewed her invitation, but the old lady shook her head.

'You've done a good job with those old roses. They were Madame Blanchard's pride and joy. She was a real woman of the land, tough and uncompromising, but I think her heart was in the right place. With a husband like she had, and four tearaway sons, she had a lot to put up with.' Once more, the old lady had drifted off into the past before pulling herself back to the present and turning to face Laura. 'It was always a beautiful spot, this garden. Peaceful. A good place to rest. I should have come earlier. Forgive me, Madame. I'm glad you've bought the old place, made something of it, given it a fresh start. Bernard, my brother, he would have liked that.'

Laura did not know what to say. She had done nothing except buy an old farmhouse and make it her home. What was there to thank her for?

'Laura - if I may – I've made some madeleines.' Madame Rossignol pulled back the cover on her trug to reveal a small, shallow plastic box with a few cakes inside. 'I thought I might go up to Madame Mini's barn and weave a while. We're behind schedule on our panel and Céline is starting to get twitchy about it. One must meet the deadline! Would you like to join me?'

***

The large wooden door to the weaving barn swung open with a creak. Sunshine streamed through the six windows between the roof beams. Madame Mini appeared to be waiting for them among the baskets of wool: red, green and gold for the autumn panels, and behind them newly hand-dyed skeins of white, grey, black and charcoal for the winter creations yet to come. Breaking all the rules, the three women sat at a trestle table dipping warm madeleines into cups of Madame Mini's tea. Inhaling the sweet, rich scent, Laura smiled and took in the great expanse of barn. Winter was not far off and the air was slightly chill. It felt to her like an empty dance studio, the echoes and space presenting a sense that anything was possible. There it was again – a feeling of happiness, even love, that Laura was not used to. It unsettled and disturbed her, and she struggled not entirely successfully to crush and destroy it. Her experience was that happiness and love ultimately led only to pain.

The three women sat in quiet companionship, savouring the taste of vanilla and sugar and the peace of the old barn. It was not long before Laura imagined her surroundings to be a darkened barn lit by the light of a single lantern. In the left of the picture there were piles of golden hay, and to the right a small red-cheeked boy, plump in his padded jacket, and a doe-eyed donkey with its ears pricked up. The child's blue pants were slit down the back in the traditional Chinese way. The image she had conjured was that of the picture that had been her penultimate and very lucrative sale. Her dealer had been ecstatic, and Bill had painted a remarkable fake, working and reworking the lighting and varnish until you could almost feel the chill of the winter night and sense the subtle heat rising from both boy and beast. Laura had adored the painting and had displayed it prominently in their lobby in Shanghai. It had prompted many admiring glances and favourable comments, all of which had served to mollify her husband for a while. A city girl born and bred, Laura still did not understand what had appealed to her about the rustic Chinese scene. Was it the way it prompted the smell of hay, muck and warmth, or was it the simplicity of another life, a rural life, and the chubby boy who was but had never been?

Very soon, Madame Mini had left. Or had she? Laura was never sure with the tapestry teacher; she seemed to appear and disappear at will. Before long, Madame Rossignol arranged her cushion on the bench in front of their loom, her movements wafting out a reassuring old-fashioned scent … What was it? Violets, perhaps? Laura sat on a stool beside her and wound butterflies of wool around her fingers to add to the pile. It was a simple, repetitive task that she enjoyed, and it speeded up the weavers' work. Madame Rossignol began filling in the oval tracings that outlined grapes in a basket. She worked carefully, using a rich purple wool that was so juicy-looking it made Laura salivate. As the old lady wove her thread into the picture, so she told her story.

'Not a day goes by when I don't think about my brothers, Maurice and Bernard. I was the youngest and I adored them. I wanted to be like them so much that for years I insisted that I was a boy! I would fight like a cat if my mother tried to put me into a dress. In the end she gave up.' Madame Rossignol produced a photograph from a small cotton bag she wore crosswise across herself. 'That's the three of us in the Santelli vineyard at harvest time. Guy sold that patch thirty years ago. It's where the new houses are; behind the post office.' She handed the photograph to Laura.

Three laughing faces looked back out of the ageing black and white, almost as if they could see out of the picture and across time. In front of them were baskets of grapes. A suntanned, fair-haired little girl in shorts, white shirt and sandals stood between the two thin boys, who were hugging her tightly. The elder one had a handsome, earnest face, more intellectual than rural farmer. His shirt sleeves were rolled up ready for work and he wore his hair slicked back in the style of the time. The younger one, still in shorts, had filthy knees and his hair fell forward over his eyes. The sun was slightly to the side of them, illuminating the unruly wisps of the boy's hair.

'Maurice was eighteen when the war began, Bernard barely eleven.' Madame Rossignol carefully put the photograph back in her bag, then worked a couple of short rows back and forth on the tapestry. As she did so, the large emerald ring on her finger glistened in the falling light. She spoke the most educated, beautiful French: the faultless eloquent grammar, the subtle rise of voice at the end of each clause, falling elegantly at the end of the sentence. It was music to Laura's ears.

'When the war began, it was all very odd, at least for the children. People in the village began to do bizarre things. There was a frenzy of burying and hiding stuff in cellars, under floorboards, in attics. France's most valuable treasure is, of course, our wine. We jolly well weren't going to let the Boche get their hands on it! My family dug up our vegetable patch and buried our best vintage and my great-grandfather's gold watch under the carrots and broad beans. The Blanchard family who lived in your house blocked up the whole of the left-hand passage of their cellar, hiding their prize wine behind it. Other winegrowers hereabouts stashed their best produce in the smaller caves high on the hill. They dug up and replanted thorn bushes in front of them so that the Boche wouldn't find them. The way it all worked out is funny. The Blanchard's cache was forgotten and not discovered until the 1970s, following a tip-off from a dying man in Saumur. What a party the village had that night! I tell you, even I got more than a little drunk! I may have stripped and danced more or less naked in the fountain! I don't mind telling you I had quite a figure back in the day…But I digress.'

'I remember very clearly the day the Germans arrived in our village. It was absurdly comical. They were five in all, led by the ugliest-looking young officer I had ever seen. My mother told me that he had a cleft lip which had been shoddily repaired when he was a child. I have never forgotten his face. Poor man, I thought, to go through life looking like that. With him were four exhausted-looking men, their boots muddy, their uniforms covered in dust and dirt. If that was an army, I did not think much of it. They accepted surrender from the mayor, hung the swastika from the Town Hall, changed the clock to Berlin time, and sped away again in the truck that had brought them. It seemed that Le Saut was nowhere of interest to them, not worth bothering with, and everyone heaved a sigh of relief when they left. But a few days later, a Weinführer arrived to audit the wine estates. That was when our war really began.

'At first, it seemed more like a game than a conflict. My brothers and other men from the village plotted to wind up the Germans. They did anything and everything to frustrate and obstruct the Germans' administration. Even we little ones learnt to fib, cheat and fob off the Boche.' 'Yes, sir, the shortcut to Tours is that way,' We'd point up the hill and over the top. In the winter their vehicles would get stuck in the mud on the single-track road on the way down! Things would go missing – bits and pieces at first – cigarette cases, lighters idly placed on a table in the bar, helmets removed in the heat and put down by the village fountain were, shall we say 'relocated'. Motorbikes would be moved – not stolen, but placed at the top of an awkward flight of steps in a corner a few streets away from where they had been left. Spark plugs would be removed from trucks, cars would get punctures, railway points would be switched, cargoes of confiscated wine bound for Germany would disappear. Barrels would be siphoned off at railway sidings. Labels would be swapped. Imagine it! When Goebbels, Göring or Von Ribbentrop opened their bottles of grand cru, only to discover cheap table wine!' The old lady chuckled. 'Yes, to begin with it was great sport. Then the Boche took our horses. Without them, how were we to plough? How were we to bring in the harvest? Then they took our cows, our chickens, our meat and finally our men. Then came the disease that ravaged our potato crop. We were hungry, always hungry, pain gnawing at our bellies. All we thought about was food. I used to dream of pork rillettes, goose pâté and bits of bacon dripping with fat. It got so bad that all the pigeons in the region disappeared, rabbits were nowhere to be found, and people even said there were no fish left in the Loire. For years afterwards I had nightmares in which my brothers were calling to me that they were hungry.'

Outside, there was laughing and chattering in the street as the village children made their way home from school. The two women rested their hands in their laps, listening, letting the happy sound flow into Madame Rossignol's story. Then she slowly raised her hands like pecking beaks to the loom to continue weaving.

'Looking back, we were all in it to a greater or lesser extent – trading, haggling for food on the black market. The war turned the whole country into a squalid nest of wrangling, haggling, lying, cheating, and wheeler-dealing. No one could say they had completely clean hands. We were starving. What good were morals and ethics then? I don't suppose old man Blanchard was worse than many others. He was just canny and had the big cellar to hide and store loot. He saw his opportunity and seized it. It turned out that Le Saut was well placed to cross the line of control that separated occupied, German-administered France and so-called Free France to the south. To cross that line, a pass was needed. This presented a golden opportunity for smuggling. Before long, Blanchard was the head of a gang of brigands running all sorts across the line. Guy Santelli's father was a good friend of my father, who was the village schoolteacher and had some standing in the community. He pleaded with Santelli not to get mixed up with Blanchard's lot, but his advice was ignored. Smuggling meat, cheese, ham, wine, guns, explosives, and people was a filthy business. In order to make it work, Blanchard collaborated with the Germans. He played a sneaky game, helping German officers and soldiers to enrich themselves while profiting himself, all the while attempting to portray himself as a patriot and a man of resistance.'

Madame Mini sighed.

'The war destroyed my family and tore our community apart. Nothing was ever the same again. The day came when my elder brother was sent for forced labour in Germany. It was a death sentence. Always a dreamer, an idealist, he fled to join the Communist Resistance. From that time onwards, my mother forbade Bernard and me from playing with the Santelli and Blanchard boys, and my childhood came to an end.'

Madame Rossignol picked up her wooden weaver's mallet and began to tap down on the plump purple grapes she had been weaving. The soft regular thump of wood on wool was reassuring, and she probably carried it on much longer than was necessary.

'Would you like me to work a little, give you a break?' Laura asked.

The old lady nodded, shifted her cushion along the bench to make room for her companion. Laura tied on a butterfly of black wool to fill in the shadow on the fruits where the old lady had left off.

Madame Rossignol sighed and rolled her shoulders; they clicked with stiffness and age.

'Towards the end of the war, fortunes began to change. Everyone knew the Germans would lose. It could only be a matter of time. Old man Blanchard attempted to shift his allegiance, to work with the Resistance and cover his tracks. One night in early spring 1944, a consignment of explosives stored in Blanchard's cellar was being transported through the village. My elder brother's Resistance group were involved, as well as my younger brother, Bernard, who was fifteen at the time. He was not like my Maurice, who was a serious, organised young man. Bernard was impetuous and thrived on risk. After years living under the German yoke, he was spoiling for a fight.

'Just you wait! I'm going to smash the bloody Germans' faces, grind their bones to dust and use them as fertiliser on our vines.' The old lady looked at the black wool butterfly she had been folding carefully around her fingers.

'It's true what they say – what is bred in the bone will come out in the flesh. Old man Blanchard was a nasty piece of work, and his elder sons were chips off the old block. Unfortunately, his partner, Santelli, was a weak man, a follower. Folk in the village had kept quiet about the gang's thuggery, partly because old Blanchard was a cunning fox and would throw the odd bone or two of black-market goods in the right direction, but also because they were frightened. Under the Nazis, they had no choice. Where was the right of redress? But when France was liberated, the tables were turned. Blanchard and Santelli saw it was their last chance, and seized the opportunity to deal with those who might give evidence against them. They betrayed the Resistance to the Nazis. When my brothers and their comrades arrived in the Blanchard's' cellar to collect the weapons, the SS were waiting for them. They were all shot.'

The silence in the barn pressed heavily on Laura, and for a second or two she could not get her breath.

'So…The voices I hear in the silence of my cellar, in the garden when the wind blows, are they real?'

Madame Rossignol nodded. Her suntanned face, wrinkled like an old apple, remained dry. Laura saw the old lady had long ago used up all her tears.

'My two brothers, and five others, two of them not even sixteen. Boys, just boys.'

It was a while before Madame Rossignol could continue, and Laura kept the silence. The light was failing faster now, but she was able to continue weaving, tenderly threading the last black shadows around the grapes until all was complete: fat, ripe, ready-to-eat grapes made of wool.

Laura wondered why this old French lady had chosen to talk to her, a newcomer to the village from the other side of the world. Had she seen something of her own grief mirrored in Laura, seen her as a kindred spirit? Certainly Laura knew all too well the anarchy of a country turned upside down, where black was white and white was black and there were no rules. It was in that moment that Laura experienced a knowing beyond understanding, that some might call love. It was a rare and precious thing that she knew was rarely gifted in life. She wanted to reach out and put her arms around the old lady and hug her tight.

'I must finish my tale,' Madame Rossignol said quietly. 'Just before the liberation, Blanchard and his family fled south. We never saw them again. Guy Santelli's father was shot dead in broad daylight by the Resistance during the purges towards the end of the war. He did not come home one Saturday night, and Guy found his father's body in their vineyard the next day, already pecked by the crows.'

Madame Rossignol sighed, then reached out and stroked the section of tapestry that Laura had just finished weaving; voluptuous-looking grapes in a basket, surrounded by loaves of bread and a round of virgin white cheese. The bench between the two women creaked as Madame Rossignol adjusted her position. Outside, it began to rain, a soft patter at first, building to a crescendo of drumming on the windows.

'Laura, if you will permit me?' Madame Rossignol addressed her companion by her given name for the first time.

Laura nodded her agreement.

'Then you must call me Alice. Madame Mini says that your coming to the village and buying the house, that this was meant to be. We don't know much about you, Laura, but Madame Mini is right. The strange thing is that ever since you came to Le Saut, worked in that garden and made the old house your home, the nightmares that have plagued me these past seventy years have stopped. Coincidence, perhaps, but I prefer to think not.' She reached out and took Laura's hand in hers.

'Alice, your hands are cold as ice!'

'Not to worry. They always are. The doctor says I have poor circulation, and that I drink too much. What tosh! I think it may be because I don't drink enough!' She smiled. 'Thanks to you, Laura, coming here to be part of our community and living in the House at the Foot of the Church, I have come to understand that it's time to forgive. I have decided to try to make it up with Guy Santelli. Why carry all my hatred and bitterness to the grave? Guy and I were friends once. Can we not be so again? God willing, it will not be too late.'

CHAPTER 19

A few weeks later, it was the dead time, three nights before New Year's Eve, when the world watches and waits. Snow had fallen that morning – a couple of centimetres at most, but the unexpected event had delighted the children who had been out all around the village, whooping and screeching, scraping up the snow to make balls and miniature men which they held up triumphantly in their hands. Eventually, darkness, stillness and peace enfolded Le Saut once more, and Laura lay snuggled under a blanket on the sofa, Boris snoozing heavily on her feet. She had lit the fire hours ago and did not need the cover, but enjoyed being swaddled; it made her feel safe. She wriggled a little, soaking up the warmth, as if the flames were nourishing her. Shadows danced on the walls. The fire crackled and spat and a large log collapsed in on itself, revealing an ancient volcanic world. With deep ravines, high peaks and golden rivers of lava, it appeared to Laura like the surface of an unknown planet far away in a distant galaxy. On the mantelpiece, the antique carriage clock she had bought at a car boot sale ticked. Closer and closer to midnight the second hand crawled forward, making its jerky rounds, until the miniature world in the fire grate dimmed and darkened, fading to softly glowing ash.

It began to get chilly in the room, but Laura was reluctant to move. If she climbed the stairs to bed, if she slept, another day would come, bringing her closer to the new year. She shivered. She had heard nothing from China, but all the same she felt the storm coming, like a distant rumble of thunder inside herself. It was as inevitable as night followed day, and it would not be long now.

Suddenly, there in the darkness, she saw her husband's face, round and young, smiling at her with his perfectly straight teeth, as if he had been expecting her. They had met at a ballet first-night party at the newly refurbished Peace Hotel in Shanghai, one of the first such occasions the ballet company had ever hosted. There he was, the tallest man in the room, nonchalantly leaning on the bar as if he were quite used to doing such things. This was impossible, of course, for such corrupt, capitalist opportunities had only been available since the implementation of the policy of the reform and opening up the country, and were a novelty to them all. He had introduced himself kindly, speaking Mandarin with the softly shushing influence of the local Shanghai dialect in his speech. Even after long years in the city, she had never got used to it; it sounded feminine to her ear. How easily their courtship had begun!

Cocooned in her blanket, Laura sighed and blinked hard in an attempt to banish the memory. It was hard to believe that she had only been free from him for just under a year, but in many ways it felt like a lifetime. In France, sheltered in her own home, she had become a different person – perhaps the person she was always meant to be. Home, she realised, was not defined by cultural background, language and country of birth; it was where you felt safe.

How could the tall, handsome, generous young man she'd married have turned into a monster? Had he always been like that, and it was just that she had failed to see it? Over the years, he had become increasingly vindictive, cruel and unpredictable. She had driven herself to the brink of madness trying to anticipate his moods and motivation so that she would not get caught out. Yet even now, she did not really understand his behaviour. How could she possibly explain it to others? If only it had been possible to rewind to the early days when the two of them used to meet in one of the new coffee shops on the Bund. He would greet her with a daring peck on the cheek which was sufficient to announce to all that she was his girl. Heads close, giggling at their behaviour, they would indulge in two frothy, milky mugs of an imported coffee and share a croissant, licking their lips and savouring its rich, buttery flavour. They had thought themselves the bees' knees, the epitome of modern Chinese sophistication. After so many years of suffering and the waste of life and talent in their country, that country was at last changing. China was modernising; the old days of 'eating bitterness' were gone. Don't look back, make money, move on! How daring the two of them had been, parading down the street holding hands, he wearing fake Levi jeans, she dangling a black Gucci handbag which he told her he had brought from Hong Kong.

How envious her friends had been! 'Wahhh! He's so charming and handsome, and he's making money. What a catch! Fei Feng, you're a lucky girl.'

His business had started small, buying electronics cheaply from factories in Fujian Province and reselling them by word of mouth in Shanghai: televisions, hairdryers, curling tongs, washing machines, toasters. He had then cautiously opened a couple of shops in the city. The modern flat he had bought off-plan over the river in Pudong had been his first foray into property. One thing had led to another, and before long the booming real estate market had become the mainstay of his business.

It was about this time that he had begun buying Chinese art. 'China's time is coming,' he told her. 'One day, the works of our unknown painters will be worth millions on the world market.' Understanding from the outset that he had little sense of culture or taste, he encouraged Laura to take charge of choosing the artworks and paintings for purchase. That would prove to be his mistake.

Laura had been happy for a while in their first apartment. What luxury it was, for neither of them had enjoyed private space before. They spent lazy Sunday mornings in bed, making love, reading books, and magazines. There was a bathroom, a shower and western flush toilet, a washing machine, and even air-conditioning in the living and bedrooms. Mostly everything worked; the only hitch was that if you ran the air conditioner and the hairdryer at the same time, the fuse blew. He would joke that a little bourgeois indulgence was fine, but not too much all at once. When they first moved in, the flat had been on the edge of paddy fields; in the early mornings before she went to ballet training, this allowed Laura to watch the workers on their bicycles pedalling to and fro, so graceful that they seemed to glide and float between the fields. They were never in a hurry and seemed to have all the time in the world. As Laura blew on her rice congee to cool it, it soothed her to see the old continuing amid the rapid modernisation of her world.

But such feelings would not last. Within a couple of years the misty, forgotten flat land on the far side of the Huangpu River had sprouted a jungle of pink and white apartment blocks with mock Grecian porticos and pillars. Laura and her husband already had more than they ever could have hoped for. Why could that not have been enough?

A smell of disinfectant welled up inside Laura. Throwing off the blanket, she jerked upright on the sofa, swallowing hard, lest she choke on her distress. She had miscarried - not once, not twice, but three times. Her last pregnancy had almost run to term, but in the final fortnight there had been no heartbeat. The baby, a little boy, had been stillborn. She had seen his face briefly, smooth and unwrinkled, eyes closed as if he were sleeping and might wake up at any moment.

The midwives had bundled him in a sheet and whisked him roughly away like a quarter-full sack of rice. 'Don't worry now. Let us deal with it. You can always have another one,' they had cooed conspiratorially, and that had been that.

The last she saw of her child was a left foot sticking out of the sheet over the sink. Five perfect toes like little pearls. The baby had never even had a name. She supposed that the body had been incinerated; in those days, people never asked. She hadn't, either.

After the baby died, everything changed between Laura and her husband. She blamed herself for their loss, guilt, pain and regret, tying knots in her mind as she tried to understand how such a tragedy had befallen them. Perhaps the years of brutal, unrelenting training at the ballet school had ruined her fertility. This, coupled with her own determination to be the best, led her to believe that nothing but perfection would do.

And after her second miscarriage, the ballet company dismissed her. Dancing had been her life. Without the camaraderie, the friends and routine, and an independent income, small though it was, Laura didn't know what to do with her life. That was when her relationship with her husband started to fall apart.

At first, they had argued about small things.

He told her he didn't like her lipstick.

'But you bought it for me,' she would respond, incredulous, wondering if perhaps it was a strange joke, as sometimes was his way.

'Don't wear so much of it, then. It makes you look like a whore. Are you a whore?'

'Don't be ridiculous. 'Of course not.'

Then: 'That dress is cut too low.'

'But you chose it with me. It's Dior.'

'Wear it only when I tell you to!'

Often it was her weight that became the focus of his dissatisfaction. 'I don't like fat lumps.' Cheeks flushed with French brandy, he would look her up and down with utter disdain.

Then he bought a set of scales and instituted a weekly weigh-in, recording her weight in the little red notebook he kept in his shirt pocket along with his Mont Blanc pen. Over time, his obsession with her appearance and weight led to the point where, every Friday evening, he refused to let her eat until she had stripped to her underwear so that he could use a tape to measure her. Only after this humiliation could they sit down at the dinner table, where he would taunt her further by pulling some dishes away from her as she reached for them with her chopsicks.

'Don't you think you've had enough? Best not to get too greedy, lest the famous prima ballerina Fei Feng grow too heavy to fly.' Throwing his head back, he would roar at his own joke.

Laura had fought back, openly at first, challenging him, arguing for reason, but this brought out the worst in him. When he used his fists, he was careful never to mark her beautiful face. A slap or a sharp whack to the side of the head would send Laura flying across the polished white marble floor. A thumping punch to the stomach would double her up, leaving her gasping for breath. After each outbreak of violence, he always said he was sorry, told her he loved her and promised he would never do it again. Then there would be presents: a dozen red New Zealand roses freighted by air, a box of Swiss chocolates in a specially insulated carrier bag so that they wouldn't melt in the steaming summer heat, a huge solitaire diamond ring, a pair of black South Sea pearl earrings. He would take her in his arms; she, stiff with fear, would turn her face away, but he would twist it back, covering it with kisses, until she surrendered. No, he wouldn't do it again. Yes, all was forgiven.

Laura had refused to give up her friends from the ballet company, people she had grown up with, who understood her without question. As her husband's business prospered, his power and influence increased. He dined in swanky new restaurants and played golf with all the locally important officials. In time, he became so powerful and influential that everyone was careful not to get on the wrong side of him. One by one, Laura's true friends distanced themselves, moved abroad, or quietly slipped out of her life, to be replaced by his business associates, friends from his club and local party members.

In the end, only two of Laura's real friends remained. Little

Swan – now married and with a son – had become a teacher at the ballet school; Laura's long-term dance partner, Bin, had given acclaimed performances in New York, London and Sydney, and she felt happy that he had achieved international success. Everyone said that it was such a shame Laura had retired. She and Bin had been a dance partnership made in heaven, mesmerising to watch on stage, each anticipating and accommodating the subtlest motion of the other, and dancing as if they were one. And yes, they had loved each other. They had done so since the first time Teacher Wang had partnered them together as blushing fourteen-year-olds, when they'd had to hold hands. But it was a platonic love between two artists. Laura was one of the very few people who knew that Bin was gay. That was why she knew it was so ridiculous for her husband to be jealous of him. But Laura would not betray Bin's confidence and reveal the truth, not even to defend herself from her husband's paranoid suspicion of her unfaithfulness. To do that would have destroyed Bin's career. So she had lied to her husband to cover her tracks and met Little Swan and Bin in secret, at the gym, the beauty salon, or after her English lessons. Those lessons met with her husband's approval because he wanted Laura to be beautiful, well dressed, and able to speak good English to impress and charm his friends, especially his foreign investors. She would become his trophy – a beautiful prima ballerina, now retired. She was reduced to a business asset to be managed, controlled and wheeled out when required.

Katherine Jenkins screeched louder; Laura put her hands over her ears to block out the imagined sound. He had played that track the first time he had raped her and every time afterwards. It had been high summer, and he had come home early from the office, slamming the front door behind him.

'Where are my slippers? Is my dinner ready? Not yet? Why not?' He stood there with his hands on his hips, blocking the way to the door. 'A little bird has been tweeting in my ear. You've been seeing people behind my back again. Whore!'

Holding her arms tight behind her, he'd pushed her head into the pillow until she thought she would suffocate, thrusting in hard from behind, enjoying her pain.

The following afternoon, Little Swan called, her staccato words whispered, urgently down the line.

'Are you alone? Can you talk?'

'Yes.'

'Have you heard?'

'No, What?'

'Bin was fired from the company this morning. Apparently, his performances are no longer of the standard expected. What tosh! We both know he's dancing better than ever.' Little Swan paused as if to let her runaway thoughts catch up with her voice. 'Poor guy's utterly devasted. Says it must be because he is gay. Do you know anything about it?'

In that instant, Laura's blood turned to ice. No, she had no idea. But she recalled her husband's face, iridescent with the sweat of victory, as he had rolled off her the previous evening.

'That's what happens when you go behind my back. Lie to me again, wife, and more people get hurt.'

In that instant, realisation dawned. It had been her husband who had denounced Bin to the company, pulled strings to get rid of him, to punish and control her.

Terrified, Laura had stayed with her husband, living from day to day, trying to anticipate the twists and turns of his moods, striving to be a good wife, until one weekend he beat her so badly she had not been able to leave the apartment for two weeks. They told everyone she had flu. The following month, most magnanimously, he had released her for good behaviour while ensuring he kept her passport. She was permitted to attend an international art fair in the southern city of Shenzhen.

How naïve Laura had been to think that she could escape him! The event lasted three days, but afterwards she could not face going home. For a few weeks she managed to disappear into the narrow lanes and alleys of the economic boom town, an anonymous migrant labourer like masses of others seeking a better life. She found herself a job in the kitchen of a Cantonese restaurant, and although she was not young, the boss soon realised the business potential of her startlingly beautiful face. Within three days she was promoted from dish-washer and cleaner to waitress. With no residency permit and no rights, she worked long hours for little pay. None of this she minded, for she had enough to rent a tiny room and get by. But it was not to last. Late one afternoon, just as it was getting dark, the restaurant closed early as a tropical storm was coming. Wrapped in a cheap, pink plastic cape, Laura hurried back to her room. The keepers of all the small shops were battling the rain and the rising wind to haul in their displays; cheap clothing, fake handbags, fake Hermes scarves, electronics, kitchen-ware. Behind her, a shutter banged.

Suddenly, her phone rang. Laura's heart jumped for joy: the only person who had her new number was Little Swan. She and Bin were the only people left in the world that Laura had trusted. It would be good to chat. Eagerly, she pressed the answer button on the phone, but there was none of Little Swan's familiar excited chatter. For a few ominous seconds, the line stretched taut with silence between them.

'What's wrong?'

'It's my son. Oh, God. It all happened so quickly. The man appeared out of nowhere and the next thing I knew…' Her friend's narrative collapsed into gulping sobs. 'I should never have taken him there, not at that time of day. He's such a little boy, small for his age, easily crushed.'

'Taken him where? Little Swan, calm down. What's happened?'

'Taken him to The People's Square station, of course.' Another pause as Little Swan tried to slow her breathing.

'We had gone shopping. We had such fun. Stupidly, I forgot the time, which meant we were coming back at rush hour. You know what it's like at People's Square Station at that time, hordes of people stampeding along the passages and jostling to get on the trains. We had already let one train go as it was too crowded, and were standing near to the front of the platform as the second one arrived.' Little Swan broke down again. It was a while before she could continue. 'That little boy is my life. I don't know what I would do if anything happened to him. You are my best friend in all the world, Fei Feng, I am begging you, for the child's sake, for my sake, come home.'

Laura's entire body stiffened. Her right hand, holding her phone, began to shake. The headlights of the cars and scooters whooshing through the puddles spun in front of her eyes. She saw her husband's' face, red with drink, leering down at her.

'Lie to me, wife, and people get hurt.'

The rain poured, the wind lashed at Laura's cape. She huddled in a doorway for shelter, teeth chattering.

'What happened? Tell me!'

'A man pushed my little son. He was wearing a black leather jacket and a baseball cap - I couldn't see his face. He came from behind us. He knew exactly what he was doing. It was deliberate. Quick as a flash, with two hands he shoved my child down onto the tracks. I was petrified! The look on my son's face - shock, confusion, betrayal. There was a train coming, barely one minute away. It all happened so quickly, but in my mind it was slow motion. There was not even time to scream. Another young man, a bystander, jumped down on the tracks and lifted my boy up. The two of them were hauled back onto the platform by other travellers. Thank God! If it had not been for that young man and the quick actions of bystanders, my precious boy would have been killed.'

Laura felt as though she were drowning, but again she heard her own voice, rational and reasonable as if it belonged to someone else. 'Is the little one alright?'

'Yes, fine. A bit shaken, some cuts and bruises. The fact that he's so small and light actually made it easier for his rescuers to save him. Of course, I am telling him it was just an accident.'

Here Little Swan's voice gave out, leaving the silent phone line to speak the rest, everything that they both knew but were too terrified to articulate.

The next day, Laura returned to her husband to protect those she loved, but she had learnt a brutal, important lesson: power had to be fought with power, and that meant money, lots of it, money of her own. She would endure and bide her time.

It had not been until years later, when Little Swan had died and her precious son had grown into a strapping chemical engineer, over six feet tall, and emigrated to Australia, that Laura had felt able, at last, to make her break for freedom.

***

In the grate in The House at the Foot of the Church, the embers faded almost to nothing. The room was dark and cold, and the dog snored softly. Laura got up stiffly. She did not have the heart to disturb him. Checking that his water bowl in the kitchen was full, she picked up her phone and a torch, put on her coat, hat and gloves, and slipped out of the house.

It was a crisp, clear night. Relishing the cold, she set out on the track through the woods up onto the hill. She had never done this walk without Boris, but she was not afraid. The moon was almost full; it lit her way, almost as if it had been waiting for her and was well-prepared. The light covering of snow had frosted over, and crunched under her feet. To her left and right, tree branches glinted as if touched with silver and decked with tiny crystals and pearls. Laura trod softly, not wanting to disturb the peace. In the distance, an owl hooted.

In the clearing at the top of the hill, she stopped, raised her eyes to the heavens and drank in the wonder. The sky teemed with stars – millions, billions, trillions of tiny pricks of light. Her head spun. Down was up. It was almost as if she could step out among them and pirouette along the arching bridge that was the Milky Way.

In the village below, only a few lights remained in the houses. Maddy's bed and breakfast was dark, so was the Duguets's' bar, but at Madame Rossignol's, Madame Mini's and in the presbytery, they were burning the late-night oil. As Laura watched, the light in Madame Rossignol's house disappeared, almost with a click. Standing there in the silence, Laura thought of her new friends and the crazy commemoration tapestry that had brought them together. They were working on the final winter panels. Soon it would be finished, and the new bishop was due to come at Easter. He would lead a special service during which the tapestry would be unveiled in its final place, high on the walls of the church. What would the tapestry makers do with their time then?

And then Laura thought of him, of Xavier, as she had come to know the unlikely priest – the way he listened, breathing deeply, head cocked to one side, his ugly nose that had been broken in a barrack-room fight, the tiny sun-bleached hairs on the backs of his arms and tops of his fingers that she longed to stroke. Did he know? Did he realise how much she wanted to lay her head on his broad shoulder, how she dreamed of burying her face in his thick, warm neck, breathing in the scent of him that was of candles, resting with him and in him, just a while? Laura was a fighter, bred to be strong. But she had lived so long alone.

CHAPTER 20

In the presbytery, Father Michael awoke with a start. He had left the shutters open, and moonlight streamed in through his study window. What time was it? Twenty past midnight. He had fallen asleep in his pyjamas at his desk. He had been trying to draft a homily for the Mass on New Year's Day but his heart had not been in the task. He usually worked on his laptop but had abandoned the device earlier in the evening in favour of pen and paper, in the hope that old-fashioned technology might encourage the flow of ideas. But even that strategy had failed. There was no doubt about it: he was stuck. He could go neither forward nor back until he had made a decision about his future. Deep down, he knew he had been dithering, procrastinating and evading confronting the issue for several years now. The trial of the bishop had only served to highlight the doubts and contradictions that had been gnawing at his soul. Put simply, he asked himself whether he still wanted to be, or perhaps even could be, a priest? Removing his reading glasses, he rubbed his temples, then leaned forward to put his elbows on the desk and rest his head in his hands. The decision would have to be made soon, or else he would go mad.

The troubled priest stood up and stretched, exhaling slowly. Shivering, he reached out to put on an old sweatshirt he had left on the back of the chair. It was at moments like these that he most missed his friends from the Legion, the banter, the backslapping, the bond, the trust that existed between men whose lives had depended on one another. Two of his closest friends were dead, but there were half a dozen men in the area who had served with him in various capacities over the years. When Father Michael had first moved to Le Saut, Luke had passed the word, and men had gradually emerged shyly out of the past as the priest went about his work. There was Dezo, the happy-go-lucky Senegalese security guard. Early one Saturday morning, Dezo had spotted him with his shopping trolley at the door of Super U in Saumur, and to Michael's astonishment he had sprung smartly to attention. Then there was 'Eyes', the deadly sniper probably still hiding somewhere among the vines in the next village. Tulip, a dour Dutchman, had married a French girl and they ran a Michelin-starred restaurant in Chinon. Everyone had had a nickname, even Father Michael, whom everyone called The Saint. It was extraordinary how that name would resonate with his later profession, and Father Michael chuckled at the thought of it.

Xavier, as he then was, had been on the island of Corsica for basic training with the Legion, an enraged, deracinated young man parachuting out of the back of a decrepit 1950s Nord Atlas. It was the last sortie of the day and he and his comrades had been kept hanging around all afternoon waiting to get airborne; a deliberate tactic which had given many of them the jitters. When the moment finally arrived, the sun was already setting over the Mediterranean, laying out a path of red and gold over the sea. He had been the last in line to jump. At the last second, the stocky Filipino in front of him hesitated, which meant that by the time it was his turn, the aeroplane was close to the edge of the drop zone. Xavier could see from the smoke flare that the wind might blow him into the rough ground and boulders at the foot of the mountains.

As he tumbled, he saw his angelic childhood friend, the Golden Boy and a host of his companions. They floated towards him along a pathway laid out by the setting sun. Like Xavier, they too had grown up and his golden friend was leading them, handsome and broad-shouldered in his flowing gown, his long blond hair flying behind him. Yet he still had the pure, plump face of the child. Xavier's heart ached. How he had missed him. The golden man looked at Xavier with a seraphic smile and reached out his hand. In that instant, Xavier's parachute opened, jerking him upwards, and the vision disappeared. Miraculously, the direction of the wind had changed, and Xavier landed safely right at the extreme edge of the drop zone.

Later, back at the dormitory, he was greeted with, 'Who the fuck were you waving to up there?'

'Who do you think? Angels of course!' Xavier shrugged. The remark provoked raucous, comradely laughter and a rough slap on the back. It was from that day forth that Xavier became 'The Saint.'

Father Michael thought that legionnaires had a special way about them. Once a legionnaire, always a legionnaire, and he was no exception. Over the years in the parish, this quiet band of secretive men had become a tightly knit group. They met twice a year in a small bar in a back street in Tours, sweaty bodies pressed up against each other, elbows bumping around a rickety table, laughing, joking, enjoying a few drinks and raising toasts to fallen comrades. For all of them, the highlight of their year came every autumn when they met on a local landowner's land to hunt together. The farmer's grandfather had been a legionnaire, and there was a bond of respect between men who valued the land and those who knew how to shoot, unlike others who came for the commercial shoots. Pumped up with bravado, they never left their hides and were only interested in the big prize: wild boar.

Father Michael sighed, thinking about the joy of stalking through the forest in the early autumn mist with men among whom so much was tacit yet fully understood. They hunted quietly, methodically, patiently and without dogs. Every few hours, they stopped for a bite to eat, talking sparingly as they handed around the coffee flask, the wine, the bread and the cheese. They took from the hunt only what they needed for themselves and their families, mostly partridge and pheasant, occasionally a deer, and one year a great lumbering boar. More importantly, the men were there to help each other out, often with money to tide a comrade over a difficulty of some sort. Over the years, they had supported several former colleagues who had lost their jobs; they had even helped the troublesome son of a former colleague to find work as an apprentice. Given their unwritten code of behaviour, Father Michael knew that what they did might not always have been strictly legal but that they were honest in their own way. This, he thought ruefully, was perhaps more than could be said of the Church. These were no-nonsense, straightforward men, ruffians some, who lived life by their own code, forged on the battlefield. The priest had always felt honoured to be a member of this brotherhood.

But for all that, these men could be of little help with his present dilemma, the complexities of his relationship with the

Catholic Church, his private God and his faith. The decision that confronted him about his future had to be made alone.

Through the shutters, the moon beckoned, and Father Michael moved towards the open window. The presbytery lay on the outskirts of the village, and the study window looked out on the hill. He stood in a shaft of moonlight, looking up at the stars which struggled to twinkle against the bright moon. It was then that he saw it: a tiny light floating along the top of the hill. It bobbed uncertainly, then began to descend the path that emerged behind the presbytery. Mesmerised, the priest watched. Who would be out at this time? Steadily, the light drifted downwards, getting larger by the second, and Father Michael realised it was coming for him. He had never been more certain of anything in his life.

Without hesitation, he turned his back on the window and went down the stairs. He crossed the kitchen, his plastic slippers making a flip-flopping sound on the tiled floor. As he opened the kitchen door, the security light clicked on. He stood there, watching and waiting. The light proceeded along the lane before disappearing briefly behind some taller bushes. Then it came on quickly, casting a searching beam before stopping to reveal Laura standing at the top of the garden path. She hesitated for a second or so, but this seemed to the priest an eternity. Then she crossed the garden towards him, leaving her footsteps behind her in the snow. Softly, the front door closed behind them.

She was cold in his arms. With a sigh, she laid her head on his chest, soaking up his warmth. For a long while they stood there, in the middle of the kitchen, each savouring the comfort of the other. She smelt feminine, something of roses and of frost, heavy with the chill night air. Cautiously, he put his lips to the top of her head, planting a kiss. Her woollen hat smelt of wood smoke. Slowly, he pulled it off, liberating a mass of bouncing curls. He put his index finger tenderly through a large one at the side of her head: it curled around him as if instinct had dictated it. But still, he did not have the courage to look at her face. Tipping back her chin, she raised her eyes to his, dark, wide open, questioning and answering at the same time. He smiled softly, nodding a wordless response. She removed a glove. It fell with a whisper to the floor. She placed her right hand, warm now, on his cheek. It steadied him. Cradling the back of her head in his hand, he bent forward and put his mouth to hers.

CHAPTER 21

Father Michael awoke first. The faint light of dawn squeezed around the shutters at the bedroom windows. He felt the warmth of Laura's naked body pressed up against his side. A great joy welled up inside him. He wanted to jump up, to leap and dance and sing, but he refrained for fear of waking her. Instead, he shifted his head gently to the side and rested it next to hers. She smiled a little, without opening her eyes, and snuggled closer to him.

He felt himself stir again and wondered briefly why he experienced no sense of guilt, regret or shame. But how could he? What had happened between them last night had been so beautiful. There had been no grabbing, no hurry, no haste. Neither of them was young. It had been tender, gentle and kind; in a strange way it was as if they had known each other all their lives, but it was just that they had never met before.

But who was she really, this strange woman named Laura, and what had happened to her? In their nakedness she had not been able to hide her scars, the precise punched red circles caused by deliberate cigarette burns on her thighs, the ridges that ran across her shoulders and down her back, inflicted by a whip or a stick perhaps, the deep scar behind her ear that he had felt with his fingers.

'What happened, darling? Who did this to you?'

'Hush.' She had put her finger to his lips. 'It happened in a past life. No matter now.'

The part of him that was a soldier and a priest had known from the outset that Laura was not telling him the whole truth. But the part of him that was Xavier and a man had seen enough of her over the last six months to be confident he knew the woman she was now. It humbled him that she had entrusted herself to him.

His training had taught him not to get emotionally involved. But it was too late for that. He loved this woman, and he would do whatever it took to keep her safe.

In the shadows on the far side of the room, his old duffle bag waited. He had packed it the previous day, planning to leave that morning to spend the few remaining days of the old year at the house on the Île de Ré that he had inherited from his grandmother. Now he would invite Laura and Boris to accompany him. There on the Atlantic coast, on the island where the sea meets the sky, life would be simple; they could be together, for a few days at least. As for the enormity of the implications of what had happened between them for his future in the Church - for the moment, at least, that could wait.

CHAPTER 22

Laura sat in the front seat of Father Michael's car, staring across the long bridge that led from mainland France to the Île de Ré. The sun was going down fast, setting the sky ablaze. In anticipation of the imminent darkness, the lights had come on all the way along the bridge. They appeared like beacons, leading them onwards. What lay ahead of her, she wondered? Xavier – for that was what she called him now, had explained about his grandmother's house by the sea, and she had accepted his invitation that morning. Mémé, he still affectionately called his grandmother with no trace of affection or self-consciousness. Without hesitation, Laura had washed and returned home via the hill path so as not to attract unwanted attention in the village. Once home, she had fed Boris and packed a small overnight bag. Dog and mistress had then taken the mid-morning bus to Saumur, where Xavier had been waiting for them.

Beside her, he wound down the car window and inserted his prepaid bridge toll card in the machine. She realised she had taken a leap of faith in entrusting herself to him and was now driving into the unknown. For a few seconds, her heart was in her mouth. What if she was mistaken and this enigmatic man, this legionnaire turned priest, turned out to be like her husband? Her judgement had been wrong before, very wrong. But she had been young and naïve back then; no one could describe her as that now.

The card popped out of its slot. Xavier retrieved it and the window whirred closed. In that instant, he turned and smiled in that boyish way of his that made her want to look after him, to love and reassure, to be loved in return. Softly, she slipped her hand onto his thigh, letting it rest there for reassurance. He put the car into gear, and together they drove across the bridge into the coming night. By the time they arrived at the house, it was pitch-dark. Getting out of the car, Laura took a deep breath of the salt air and turned her head excitedly, listening to the roar of the waves.

'The beach is about two hundred metres that way.' Hands full with shopping bags – they had stopped in La Rochelle to pick up three days' worth of supplies. Xavier jutted his chin into the darkness. 'We'll go tomorrow.'

Inside the house, the electric light was startlingly bright, and it took Laura's eyes a few seconds to adjust. The place was warm and expectant; Xavier had put the heating on remotely before they had left Saumur.

She was standing in a large open-plan room that had been divided according to use into three sections. It was furnished in the slightly chaotic, eccentric way of a typical French country house and was, Laura judged, pretty much as Mémé might have left it. She fell in love with the place instantly. It smelt of mothballs, an old-fashioned aroma that reminded her of her early childhood home with her parents in Tianjin, and she felt privileged to have been invited here. The middle part of the room contained a heavy, shiny-topped wooden table, set for ten. Against the wall, an old-fashioned dresser towered above it; the top section was glass-fronted and filled, somewhat haphazardly, with an assortment of different-sized wine and liqueur glasses, brightly coloured bowls, serving platters, and bottles of alcohol. To the right of the dining area lay the kitchen, the sliding doors to which had been left open. On the other side of the dining table was the sitting room. Laura carried her holdall into this space and put it down. There was a saggy-looking three-seater sofa decorated in a faded red-and-gold paisley, flanked by two trendy two-seaters that looked as if they might have been purchased from IKEA. Pride of place was given to a high-backed armchair which sat to the right of the fireplace. On its top lay a carefully placed lace antimacassar. It was as if Mémé was sitting there waiting for them, and Laura saw her in her mind's eye. She was wearing a black dress adorned only with a diamanté brooch which twinkled in the light. Her tiny face was deeply suntanned. Putting her hands on the arm-rests to steady herself, the old lady got up and smiled Xavier's impish grin.

'Welcome, my dear.'

Shaking the vision from her head, Laura crossed over to the kitchen, where Xavier was already starting to make a meal. Boris lay contentedly at his feet, tapping his tail from time to time on the linoleum. Without a word, she washed her hands, and began to help. With a soft kiss on the cheek, he passed her a chopping board and a knife, asking her to chop carrots. He was already sautéing onions in a frying pan.

'What are we making?' she asked.

'Spaghetti Bolognese.' He shrugged apologetically. 'It's quick and easy.'

Before long he had added the mince, spices and a generous glug of wine. As Xavier worked, the fatigue and worry seemed to fall off him. He moved more easily, the furrows on his brows retreating, the line of his mouth relaxing. It was almost as if he were shedding a skin, the priest becoming a man. Occasionally, he would raise his eyes from his task, looking for her, and when his eyes met hers, there would be a look of wonder and amazement that filled her with joy. What had she done to deserve such bliss? Was not love reserved for the young?

The water for the pasta began to boil. Leaning on the kitchen worktop, arms around each other, they watched and waited, feeding each other crisps and sipping wine from one glass.

'Don't think too far ahead!' Laura warned herself. They had these few days together before New Year, when Xavier had to be back in his parish. She knew she was being reckless with herself and with him also, but for the moment, the joy of the present was overwhelming. She did not have the strength to turn away.

***

The following morning, they arose late. Ravenous, they ate a large brunch. Laura fried Chinese-style omelettes with spring onions, which they followed with croissants and fresh fruit. Afterwards, they wrapped themselves in coats, scarves, hats and gloves and set out for the beach.

The house lay behind sand dunes and a barricade of pine trees which protected it from the worst of the Atlantic winds. Barking gleefully, happy to be off the leash, Boris charged ahead of them along the sandy path through the trees. Sharing in his delight, Laura and Xavier ran after him down to the beach where the tide was out. Halfway across the expanse of sand,

Boris stopped to check that Laura and Xavier were following him, his tongue lolling out of his mouth, then he was off again. Catch me if you can!

Jubilant, all three of them arrived at the water's edge. There they stood, and Laura licked her lips, relishing the taste of salt on the spray. The winter light played tricks, and an onlooker standing in the pines would not have been able to see the couple, for they had been swallowed up by the blinding blue dazzle. The rolling waves crashed and the wind whisked streaks of cloud and whipped the sea into a chaotic frenzy, blurring shape, form, definition and line.

After a while, holding hands, the couple turned, and they and the dog began to walk along the deserted beach in the direction of the village. Xavier had picked up a stick for Boris from among the pines; at intervals, he threw it for the dog to chase. Getting up his courage and not seeming to mind the cold, Boris chased in and out of the pebble-rattling, foaming shallows. This in turn encouraged the couple, who let the weakened incoming waves hiss at their feet. Buffeted by the wind, Laura and Xavier lifted their arms like children, as if they might fly. As they approached the village, the beach got a little busier, and they stopped their games. Laura judged it prudent to withdraw her hand from the priest's. Shapes emerged out of the crystal blue: a stocky man whose knees turned outward, wearing wellington boots; a grandmother with a child in a yellow raincoat carrying a bucket and spade; and a young man riding a surfboard on wheels with an orange sail, who whizzed along the wet sand. Hidden behind the sand dunes, only the top of the spire of the village church was visible from the beach.

'Want a coffee?' Xavier asked, pointing to a small wooden shop at the top of a concrete slipway where a lone seagull circled. It was a coffee shop selling ice cream, hot dogs, waffles and crêpes. In the summer it would have been thronging with customers. There were only a few people coming and going that day, but seemingly enough to make opening worth the owner's while.

Laura nodded.

Having bought their coffee, they returned to the beach and sat on the leeward side of the slipway. It was a relief to no longer battle the wind. The coffee steamed, and the concrete was almost warm on their backs. Removing their hats and gloves, they lifted their faces to the sun. Laura took out some of the trophies she had collected at the water's edge and laid them on the sand: a couple of shells and a piece of bright, green sea glass which glinted like a dragon's eye. She looked at Xavier; the tip of his nose was red from the cold, but he was staring along the beach into the haze of light as if looking for something or someone.

'I have spent some of the happiest days of my life here on this island. This place gifted me something when I was very young. It's taken me years to understand, but it's where it all began.'

Laura had no need to ask what he meant. She understood that he was referring to his faith.

'When I was a child, my mother used to send me here to spend my holidays with Mémé. In those days there was no bridge, so we came over by ferry. I'd be so excited! I'd have the whole long summer to run free. Mémé used to take me everywhere with her, and there was no such thing as bedtime! We had such adventures, cycling all over the island, collecting wild flowers, eating picnics, building dens in the garden and watching the birds. I had a little imaginary friend I used to play with. I called him the Golden Boy, because that is how he appeared to me. Real or imagined, I loved him. He was so beautiful and kind. In all the years I knew him as a child, he never spoke a word. I could tell him anything, and he would keep my secret.

'One windy summer day, the two of us were building a sandcastle, right there.' Xavier pointed to a spot just below the slipway. 'Mémé was nearby, collecting shells for me to decorate my construction with. Suddenly the Golden Boy in my mind's eye stood up and pointed to a group of about half a dozen golden children of a similar age playing in the sunshine by the water's edge. Smiling, he gestured for me to follow. Naturally, I did not hesitate, and sprinted after him down to the water's edge, or rather, I ran and the Golden Boy floated, for he had wings. But the closer I got, the further away the other golden children seemed to be. I tried to catch up, but the faster I ran, the more they drifted away, so that by the time I got to the water's edge they were far out at sea, dancing above the waves, wings unfurled. Without thinking, I splashed into the waves, deeper and deeper, until the water was up to my waist. I wanted so much to play with the golden children, to be part of the gang. Then I heard Mémé shouting, shrieking, desperately calling for me to stop. I was losing my footing, and the water was beginning to drag me away. At the last moment as a large wave was about to break over me, I felt the Golden Boy lifting me by the shoulders and pulling me back to the beach, where Mémé fished me out, shivering and gasping for air. She held me tight in her arms, rocking me. The waves crashed onto the beach, and the two of us stared out to sea, just like you and I are doing now. The golden children were fading into the sunshine, leaving a trail of tiny silver stars.'

'Look,' I said, pointing to my vision, not expecting her to share it, for no one else ever could.'

'Yes, my love, they are the angels.'

'You can see them too, Mémé?'

'Yes, my love. I can.'

'I was astonished, for Mémé also saw into my world. That was the first time in my life I knew I was not alone.'

Then Xavier laughed and shrugged bashfully, as if to dismiss his ramblings. 'It was all so long ago.'

Laura did not think, as others might, that he was mad; rather, she saw that this was his way of expressing the great unknown and interpreting the natural world.

He stood up, dusting the sand off himself. 'Shall we go into the village? We can walk back by the road. It will be more sheltered that way.'

'Is that wise?' Laura asked, fearful that people who knew him might talk.

Again he shrugged, but this time his jaw tightened. 'Maybe not. But I don't care.'

The village was a collection of blue-shuttered, low-rise white buildings in the style typical of the region and centred around a small market square. As they walked in, the winter sun was disappearing fast behind a bank of clouds rolling in from the sea. There was a sense of gathering gloom and for a brief moment, Laura felt as if the two of them had been shipwrecked and had washed up in a ghost town. The butcher's, bakery, travel agent's, café and cycle hire shops all were shuttered. In the middle of the square stood the plain white church. *Our Lady of the Annunciation*, the plaque outside announced.

'Is it open? Shall we go in?' Laura was shocked to hear herself ask. For as long as she could remember, she had avoided churches because of what had happened to her mother.

Even Xavier looked surprised. 'Probably, if you like.'

Together they climbed the stone steps to the entrance, and Xavier lifted the latch on the heavy wooden door. 'Are you sure?'

Laura had no voice to reply, but nodded. Stepping over the threshold, she braced herself internally, anticipating the barrage of crippling emotions she expected to experience. Instead, she stepped into a place of silence and stillness, and her mind was calm.

The church was of medium size and without gaudy decoration; the beams black, the walls whitewashed, the windows without stained glass. But it was more beautiful, Laura thought, because of its simplicity. Their footsteps echoed as they walked down the nave towards the front of the church, and they sat down next to each other in a pew on the left-hand side. She thought that Xavier might bow his head to pray, but he did not.

They sat in silence for a long time, enjoying the peace. It was as if the whitewashed walls were porous and soothing away her pain. She felt Xavier's hand on top of hers; he had removed his glove and his hand was warm.

'I cannot become a Christian,' Laura whispered, turning her head to look him in the eye.

His reaction was not what she had expected. His face seemed to age twenty years, collapsing in on itself with shock and distress.

'Never, my love. You must not. It is not something I would ever want for you or ask of you.'

'My love', two words, effortless now, that meant the world. No one had ever called Laura that since she was a small child, and his simple gift of the two words to her made her weep.

CHAPTER 23

The following day there was no wind, and the sun had lost its early-morning battle against the clouds. Again, Laura and Xavier rose late, but this time they set out on bicycles, two figures on the paths that ran through the salt marshes. It was as if time had stood still, everything frozen by the frost that had come down overnight. They did not talk, for they did not want to disturb the peace and were content in the stillness. This flat wilderness on the edge of the sea reminded Laura of paddy fields, and she felt as if life had brought her full circle. Every now and then a bird would call, its voice magnified by the great expanse of sky. Laura began to draw pictures in her mind, happy memories she would treasure and return to another day. Colours were precious on the wintery margins; eagerly, she sought them out, the hints of blue and purple against the backdrop of grey, the startling red of an abandoned wheelbarrow against the white piles of salt, the stark black outline of a tumbledown shed. Every once in a while they stopped to rest, sipping coffee from a flask, Xavier's breath warm and sweet close to her ear as he handed her the cup.

Occasionally he would take out a pair of binoculars. 'Look!' He would pass them to her, his gloved hand brushing against hers, and Laura would listen as he named the birds. The unfamiliar words sounded like poetry to her. For once, she did not attempt to learn or memorise them, content to observe the turn of Xavier's head and enjoy the lilt of his voice. And yet, she sensed the turmoil in his mind, that he too, like her, was running away from something.

Was it a shared sense of doubt that had drawn them together? Did they have a future together - and if they did, was she willing to embrace it? Tomorrow they would return to Le Saut, and it would be difficult to avoid the awkward questions. Laura stared at the piles of white salt and grey landscape. Out on the marshes that winter's day, there was no perspective, not a scrap to be had. They were two tiny souls lost between the sea and the sky.

***

After supper, Laura and Xavier sat snuggled together on the sofa. They had lit the fire and were warm and relaxed, sipping wine. Laura sensed that he might be on the cusp of giving up the priesthood for her, and the thought of him making such a choice terrified her. She had not told him that she was married, legally at least. She wanted to tell him the truth right there and then, but feared ruining what had been the happiest few days of her life. It would be better to leave the confession until they got back to Le Saut.

Instead, she caressed his shoulder, and asked him a different question. 'Not long after we met, you told me how the boy became a man. You have never told me the rest of the story; how the soldier became a priest.'

If she thought he might be irritated by the question, she was wrong, for he just chuckled a little and got up to lay another log on the fire. Then, settling back with Laura's head resting against his shoulder, Xavier looked into the flames and began his tale.

'Thinking back, the idea of taking holy orders had been dormant in me for a long time. Even in my wild years, I would pray when no one was looking and went regularly to Mass. People of a religious bent say that it is like a calling, a still small voice inside that must be answered. That's true. I think I had heard it within me ever since I was a small boy. It was like a bubbling song of joy deep in my belly, but I chose to ignore it. Bizarrely, it was the senseless brutality of the Bosnian War that made up my mind.'

Xavier took a deep breath and sipped his wine.

'In January of 1993 the regiment was deployed to guard Sarajevo Airport as part of the United Nations Protection Force. The once beautiful city, surrounded by mountains, was under siege by the Serbs. In some places the two sides were dug in in First World War-style trenches only yards apart. The whole scene was like something from a post-apocalypse movie: shelled skeletons of buildings, burnt-out cars, roadblocks, a red Coca-Cola sign suspended between charred lamp posts, and the civilian population living in squalor in basements. The agreement through which the Serbian authorities handed over the airport to UN control stated that it must be used exclusively for the transportation of aid for the civilians trapped in the city. Night after night the city was shelled, so that there was never any peace. The winter was bitterly cold with snow, and the civilians were engaged in a daily battle for survival. Every time someone stepped outside for food, water or firewood they risked a sniper's bullet.'

Xavier stopped and ran his hands over his head, as if smoothing down the hair that was no longer there. 'It is difficult to describe the scale of death and destruction, the magnitude of senseless human suffering. We were witnessing a medieval siege of a modern city on the fringes of the European Union. The regiment had been through Operation Desert Storm and served in conflict zones in Africa. We were not new to warfare, but in those places we could at least flatter ourselves that we were the good guys. None of us was prepared for what we encountered in Sarajevo. We did what we could to help and protect civilians, but we were peace-keepers and for a long time had no mandate to intervene, even when snipers were targeting civilians. We worked with our hands tied behind our backs. Every night, hundreds of people would try to escape the besieged city across the airport. It was our duty to round them up and release them back to the city. Night after night we would put on our night-vision goggles and drive our armoured personnel carriers out into the killing zone. When we saw civilians making a run for it - often they were women and children - we would slow our vehicles to walking pace to try to give them some protection from the snipers' bullets. But the shooters were merciless. They would aim underneath the vehicle to hit people's legs and feet, so the civilians would huddle against the large tyres of the vehicle to try to avoid being shot. Despite our best efforts, many died or sustained terrible injuries. Day after day, night after night, month after month, the noise of shelling and crackling of gunfire never let up, and the bodies piled up. It was a living hell.

'Witnessing such things…, it gets to people after a while. Some of the younger men turned to me for comfort and support. They would come quietly and sit a while. At first, I was perplexed. But in time, I realised they wanted something from me that they did not have themselves. I was humbled and terrified at the same time.'

Xavier stopped again to sip his wine.

'Late one freezing afternoon, I was out in an armoured personnel carrier on a mission in the city. Suddenly a well-dressed woman walked out from behind a carpet that was strung across the gap between two buildings as a screen from snipers' bullets. She was wearing high heels and a smart coat with a pink-and-white scarf tied jauntily around her neck. She carried a bag in her right hand, and I thought perhaps she was trying to cross the street to a vegetable patch on the other side. She made no attempt to run or duck but simply strolled out, proud and tall, right into the line of fire. Instinctively, we slowed our vehicle to try to give her protection, but it was too late. For a few seconds we thought we might get to her before the sniper did. Sometimes they played roulette with their victims. Then – crack! – the bullet came, and she collapsed like a rag doll in front of our windscreen. What I did next was madness. I ordered the vehicle to stop at the side of the body and jumped out. A hail of bullets clanged off the side of the vehicle, one grazing my head. I pulled the woman into the back of the vehicle. She was still alive, but only just. I shouted, "Drive!" and we set off at pace along the potholed road to the hospital.'

'The bullet had gone into her upper chest, just above her heart. I found the exit wound and put a field dressing on. At this point she grabbed my hand and held it in hers, patting it as if comforting me. She muttered something I did not understand, but I saw that something in her eyes. It's difficult to describe – she was in great pain, and yet there was a peace, a knowing, an understanding. The vehicle bumped and juddered, but miraculously her face was almost serene. I sat with her, holding her hand. Without knowing why, I began to pray. Probably she was a Muslim, but it did not matter. She smiled approval at me and nodded, then closed her eyes.

'By the time we got to the hospital, she was dead. As we removed her body and put her in a body bag, the sun was setting over the building and mountains, burnishing the sky in a glory of red and gold. What made that woman walk out like she did? Perhaps she had lost loved ones and was the only one left. Perhaps she had given up caring – but at that moment, as I stared up at the blazing sky, I knew she was at rest. I thought then that being with this stranger in her final moments was the most important thing I had ever done in my life… You must think I'm mad, with all this and the angels as well.'

'No,' Laura said, shaking her head and smiling.

The fire crackled, and Boris snuffled at the foot of the sofa.

'So that's when you decided to become a priest?'

'You might ask, how can one find God amid the carnage of war? But that's just it. When all is lost, when we are reduced to nought, in the emptiness, that is when we find it, a kernel of eternity.' Slowly, he curled his right hand into a fist as if plucking something invisible out of the air and enfolding it. Then he chuckled self-consciously and shrugged. 'All we have is each other, and it's the sharing that makes life bearable. God for me, it's not the Church - it's life.'

Laura smiled and said quietly, 'It is a great gift that you have, to bring comfort to people. You must not give up your ministry for me. I am not worth it.'

But Xavier was staring into the blazing fire, lost in thought, and did not respond.

In that instant, Laura realised that she must leave Le Saut, but not because of what he had just told her. No – she loved him all the more for it. Going would tear her apart, but to stay risked destroying this wonderful man and the odd assortment of villagers who, despite themselves, had taken her in and become her friends.

CHAPTER 24

It was a month or so later when they came for Bill Winston. Alone in the cabin, he had risen early, brewed himself a strong cup of tea, put more logs into the burner, and thrown open the shutters to wait for the light. As dawn broke, he picked up his brush. The final stage of the painting had come together in his mind late the previous night. It was a large canvas, an abstract of a frozen river tributary high in the mountains. Exhilarated by the vision and terrified that inspiration might desert him, he had given himself only a few hours' sleep. Now he was nearly done, he worked at pace, adding the finishing touches to the dagger-sharp shards of purple ice. The composition radiated a savage, cruel, cracking cold, and despite the fire, he shivered with anticipation and excitement. It was an ethereal work that captured the brutal beauty of the Canadian winter, and he knew it was one of the best canvases he had ever painted.

Bill was so lost in concentration that he did not hear them until it was too late. Car doors slammed and he looked up through the window. Three men had got out of a Toyota truck. In that instant, he realised he had seem two of them before, in late fall; they had loitered at the back of the shop, raising his suspicions. Now, as then, they wore black puffa jackets and

New York City baseball caps, but it was the imperious turn of the head and their trademark swagger that gave them away. Hired Chinese thugs, who had grown too big for their boots. Did they think they owned the world? He ought to have taken more precautions to hide his identity. How could he have been so stupid?

A tall man got out of the front passenger side of the truck, towering a full head above his companions. Unlike them, he wore a smartly tailored navy city coat and was bareheaded. Bill's heart thumped in his chest. Everyone in Shanghai knew this man: the famous businessman and philanthropist, Zhang Wu – Fei Feng's husband.

Bill's mind raced. If Zhang Wu had come for him, it meant he had discovered the scale of the art fraud Bill and Fei Feng had perpetrated; she had masterminded an incredibly successful illegal enterprise that had funded both their lives outside China. Bill was surprised – but, now it came to it, not surprised. Deep down, he had always known that this day would come. It was amazing that they had got away with it for so long.

Bill must have moved at the window; for Zhang Wu was already pointing to him and shouting orders to his men. Bill dithered. He had a decision to make. Should he attempt to save himself and bar the door, or find his phone and warn Fei Feng? He did not have the time to do both.

He chose his muse.

Men were running; footsteps thumped on the veranda outside. There was a shattering sound as icicles fell from the gutter around the porch roof. Bill grabbed his phone, hand shaking as he scrolled through his email address list.

'FF' for Fei Feng: there it was. He fumbled with the characters on the virtual keyboard. Running, footsteps continued to pound on the wooden porch. Hastily, he scanned the Chinese phonetic virtual keyboard to tell Fei Feng that her husband had arrived, but there was no time. It threw up the character for 'knife' as the men barged through the unlocked door.

'Get him! Mother-fucker!'

At the last second, Bill chose the knife, but the phone was whacked out of his hand. It went flying across the cabin, then a fist landed in his face.

Had he hit send?

Bill tried to steady himself but fell backwards against the easel. Roughly, two of the thugs hauled him up and pulled his arms backwards, almost ripping them out of their sockets.

'Enough!' Bill heard Zhang Wu bark. 'Let him up.'

Bill reasoned that there was no point in struggling and allowed the men to manhandle him to a wooden chair, where they sat him down. Zhang Wu was standing with his back to the log burner, surveying the portrait of Fei Feng, her smouldering black eyes, naked shoulders and hair flying loose in the wind. The other two men were also staring, drinking her in.

'So you're the artist?' Zhang Wu sneered, looking down at Bill. 'I believe we've met once before, on the waterfront in Shanghai, many years ago. Not bad, not bad at all' – he jutted his chin back at the portrait, 'if you like painting whores.'

Bill Winston stared defiantly back at him.

Pulling up another wooden chair, Zhang Wu unbuttoned his coat and sat down, crossing his long legs one over the other. He was wearing new-looking brown suede brogues. Footwear that was quite unsuitable for a Canadian winter.

'Cosy place you've got here, Mr Winston,' he sneered.

Zhang Wu was a handsome, charismatic man, the type of person who could turn charm on and off at will. He had aged well, his looks enhanced by well-cut grey hair and expensive clothes.

'Where is she, then?'

'Who?'

Bill instantly regretted playing innocent, for he received another punch, this time in his stomach.

Zhang Wu waited for him to regain his breath. 'Don't play games.'

'I don't know,' Bill said – and really, he did not. The only contact he'd had with Fei Feng had been several years ago, and that had been via her email address in the Cayman Islands, the one he had tried to use to warn her just now.

'Get his phone,' Zhang Wu commanded. One of his men picked it up from the far side of the room and handed it to Bill.

'Unlock it.'

'I will not.'

Bill took another blow hard to the side of his face, and tasted blood.

'Enough!' Zhang Wu ordered. Slowly, he took out a metal nail file and began to tend his nails, letting the silence work its own torture.

Bill's teeth began to chatter with fear. He tried to bite down to contain the reflex, but could not, and soon his whole body was shaking.

'Where is she?' Zhang Wu asked. 'Fei Feng.'

'I don't know. Truly, I don't.'

Zhang Wu raised his hand just in time to stop one of the thugs hitting Bill again. I haven't got time for this.' Stowing his nail file and taking out his phone, he called a number. He put it on speaker so that Bill could hear.

'You've got her?'

'Yes, boss.'

'Go to video.'

'Live now.'

Standing up, Zhang Wu removed his coat, folded it and put it over the back of the settee. Next he carefully took out a packet of cigarettes and lit one from a silver lighter. Tipping back his head and puffing smoke towards the ceiling, he handed his phone to one of his men.

'Show him!'

The connection was poor. Bill heard her voice first – crackling, broken, distressed.

'Dad? Dad! Is that you? Make them stop! Please make them stop!'

'Melissa, is that you?' Bill was incredulous – but then the video came on. His daughter, dressed only in her underclothes, was propped up against the pillows of her bed in her apartment in Edmonton. Her arms and feet were bound in front of her, and her pretty face was red and swollen with tears.

'Bastard! Fucking *bastard*!' Now Bill Winston fought, jumping up in his chair, kicking, screaming, punching wildly at his captors. 'Leave my daughter alone!'

This time it was Zhang Wu himself who punched Bill in the face, and when his victim fell to the floor, he kicked him twice in the belly. Bill heard Melissa screaming as they hauled him back into the chair.

'Such a pretty girl. Fit, too!' Zhang Wu unfolded a white handkerchief and wiped Bill's blood off his knuckles. 'My men are all pumped up, ready to take a turn with her. I wouldn't mind a go, either.'

Bill Winston gasped. 'There are laws in this country.'

'Laws, is it?' Zhang Wu threw back his head and laughed. 'Laws,' says the thief. Did you think you and that gutter-slut wife of mine could embezzle me out of millions of dollars of art and that there would not be consequences? Did you fuck her as well? Was she good? Lazy bitch, she likes it rough.' He licked his lips and bared his teeth. 'Where is she, Fei Feng? Tell me, and your daughter will be unharmed.'

'I don't know where she is! Truly I don't!'

'Strip the girl,' Zhang Wu ordered into the phone.

They thrust the device in front of Bill's face. 'Come on, lads, let's watch!'

Melissa screamed.

'Stop! Wait!' Bill yelled. 'Let me think. It's true I don't know where Fei Feng is, but I know where she might be. Call your men off and let my daughter go!'

Zhang Wu took the phone, switched off the speaker, and spoke rapidly into it. 'Get some clothes on the bitch. If you haven't heard from me within ten minutes, let her go.' With that, he switched off the device and put it back in his pocket. 'So,' he sneered. 'Where is she?'

Bill spat blood in the direction of Zhang Wu and looked the man in the eye.

'France, I think she will be in France. Fei Feng loved the French language, art and history. She spoke French, learnt it in secret. Did she ever tell you her real father was French?'

And in that moment, Bill Winston had his victory. It was manifest in the look of utter incredulity on Zhang Wu's face, followed by a dawning realisation: the woman he had abused and attempted to control had had a life of her own.

It was two weeks later when Bill Winston's body was found at the bottom of the ravine, near the river he had so lovingly painted. He must have slipped on the ice, fallen, and broken his neck. The strange thing was that his body had been left untouched by the wild animals.

CHAPTER 25

Laura was sitting in front of a central loom in Madame Mini's studio. Every second was precious to her, the bobbin heavy in her hands. She worked meticulously, aiming for perfection with each stitch as if this strategy might hold back time. Xavier too had come to weave that evening, and sat in his cassock in front of the loom at the far end of the row. If Laura raised her eyes, turned her head a fraction and looked through the lines of weft, she could see his face reflected in the corner of a neighbouring weaver's mirror. Xavier and Laura did not look at each other directly, but she knew that he could see her in the same way. At times, his eyes rested upon her. Every move she made she sensed reflected in his.

The vast room was silent, thick with concentration, but Laura's heart raced. How could the others not hear its heavy thump? How could they not see the connection between her and the priest? In her mind, it was as visible to all as if someone had stretched bright-red thread across the room and bound them together.

They were cautious now, meeting only for morning walks and twice when Xavier had come to The House at the Foot of the Church under the cover of darkness. The final tapestry nearly finished. Laura felt it, tight like strings binding her heart. Sooner or later they would be found out.

Glancing again through the lines of weft into her own mirror, Laura measured the position of the leafless black tree she was weaving. The final part of the tapestry was far and away the most ambitious part of the project; Madame Mini had carefully graduated techniques for her novice weavers, leaving the most challenging ones until last. Woven in a modern, monochrome style, the apparent simplicity of this piece belied its complexity. The composition of blacks, charcoals, greys and whites had to be exact – all the more so since, unlike the other seasons, the winter pieces were designed to sit together as a single scene depicting the village in winter with a view up onto the escarpment. Despite the technical difficulties, the villagers had been determined to make their final tapestry a success and were all of the opinion that it was their best piece.

For a second or two, Laura let her eyelids flicker upwards to catch the reflection of the priest's face, impassive in contemplation. She could feel the scratch of his whiskers on her cheek and blinked quickly, as if taking a photo of him that she might carry with her forever. She had already overstayed in Le Saut, and knew it was increasingly dangerous to tarry. She ought to have left straight after New Year, but had not been able to tear herself away.

'Tomorrow,' she said every morning, and yet another day passed without action. She avoided checking her email and switched off her phone. On the long dark evenings when she was alone, she escaped into books, beautiful stories of myths, magic and long-lost lands. Perhaps just a few days longer? What harm could it do? But already the nights were drawing out. Just the other day she had even heard a blackbird sing, and the tapestry was nearly finished. Looking around the room, she could see the sections of exposed weft decreasing apace with every new stitch. There would be two or three more sessions at most, and the work would be done. Then Laura would no longer have an excuse to stay. The time had come.

Who was she now? Not the person she had been a year ago, that was certain. She had changed, and most of the time she was free of pain; time, her garden, the tapestry, the dog, her new friends and, most of all, Xavier had seen to that. It was not that the pain was gone – she understood that - rather, it was that freedom and change meant she was able to rise above it. Of course, she was Chinese, and always would be. The thought of her homeland stabbed at her heart, but there was nothing left for her there now. Her parents, her friends, all were dead, thanks to her husband and the Party. And yet she was not French, either, although she had made a home, a new life and love in this beautiful place.

Of one thing she was certain: her husband was a man who could never lose. He would come to exact revenge, and it would be a terrible thing. There were only two ways out, and she would not let him hurt her friends. Never again. That left her with only one choice.

The sooner she started her preparations, the better. She would wait until the first swallows returned, then she would steel her heart and leave. She knew that the moment she left, her pain would return, but nothing was free in life. There was always a price. She would disappear overnight; no explanations, no farewells. It would be safer for all concerned.

She thought of the bulbs she had carefully planted in her garden last autumn, dormant still but plump with promise; of the brightly coloured packets of seeds she had purchased, ready for the spring – carrots, chillies, courgettes, tomatoes, lettuce. She would have had such a bumper crop. She had maintained good relations with the estate agent in Saumur and could sell the house at a later date; rent it, perhaps. Her lawyer in Lisbon could handle the finer details. But where would she go? She had no idea. Poland, Hungary, North Africa, South America perhaps, somewhere she could slip into another world. But wherever she went, it would not be the life she now wanted with Xavier. She felt dizzy and sick. She shot a glance at her lover in the mirror, then quickly closed her eyes in an attempt to suppress her emotions. It took all her strength not to cry out. Why had she been so foolish as to give herself to this man?

CHAPTER 26

The night before the verdict was due to be returned in the bishop's trial, Xavier had been unable to pray. Instead, he sought God in the amber nectar of a couple of glasses of Armagnac. He slept fitfully, awaking before dawn feeling battered and bruised as if he had been in a drunken brawl. He arrived early in Angers for the morning court without having eaten breakfast. They were in the middle of a March heat-wave, and the morning was already warm, the sky a startling blue, full of spring promise that hurt his eyes.

Having parked the car, he found a café bar in a side street not far from the courthouse. It served the institution's needs and was already bustling with morning trade. There was only one unoccupied table remaining, to the left of the entrance. It wobbled on the uneven pavement as Xavier sat down. He felt gawky and twitchy disguised in his civilian suit with a tie rolled up in the pocket, bizarrely agitated as if he were a boy again in the presence of his father. He could not remember the last occasion he had worn a suit and tie, but that morning was not a day to advertise his profession. What a coward he was, he thought. He balled and un-balled his hands, breathing in the aroma of fresh coffee and illegal, but ever so tempting, cigarette smoke. God, he was dying for a fag, but he had given up when he left the regiment. He knew Laura was trying to abstain too, so he held off, more for her sake than his own.

A bored-looking waiter appeared at his side, dressed in black shirt and trousers; he was unshaven, his hair dishevelled and the laces of his trainers locked in multiple knots, evidence that he habitually just slipped them on. Xavier always noticed people's shoes – a product of his years in the regiment – but these days he did his best not to judge. The lad bent down and shoved a piece of folded cardboard under the leg of the table to steady it. The order was placed in the time-honoured way, via a few grunted words and a couple of nods with the minimum of pleasantries: black coffee and a chocolate croissant. Xavier had seen some in a basket on the bar, a concession to modernity probably forced by competition from Starbucks.

Leaning back in his chair, Xavier stretched his legs out onto the pavement in the direction of a couple of scruffy city pigeons. They didn't give a damn about the intrusion and carried on pecking about. The café was old France, the tables grimy, all slightly down at heel, but it was the France he knew and loved, the one he trusted. Occupying the tables directly in front of Xavier was an odd assortment of men and women of all ages, clearly journalists and film crew who had come to report on the trial. Many knew each other and greeted one another with four kisses on the cheek. There was a balding middle-aged man in a shabby suit, his belly bursting at the buttons of his shirt: he was staring into his laptop and slurping his coffee at the same time. The glamorous female reporter next to him stroked on thick layers of vermilion lipstick, pouting into a compact mirror. The heels of her black patent shoes were so high that Xavier doubted she would be able to walk in them. The camera crew were all dressed in jeans, sweatshirts and baseball caps and joked quietly among themselves. Meanwhile, court workers came in a steady stream to get their morning fix of caffeine, some with badges around their neck. Behind him, Xavier could hear the boss greet them by name with heavily accented Algerian French, which made him feel homesick for the diversity of the Legion. Most workers hurried away with their coffee in paper cups. Some, however, congregated at a table to Xavier's left that had been placed a little outside the awning. The strategy was deliberate, perhaps so that they could smoke and not technically be within the precinct of the café? The rest of the tables were taken by people whom Xavier identified as 'civilians' – witnesses and victims, perhaps, and their families. Three no-nonsense-looking women and men who were probably their husbands, hunched at one table. Their lives had not been easy, the stresses and strains etched into their faces. Next to them was an aloof-looking blonde-haired lady dressed in an elegant double-breasted trouser suit and white crocodile leather shoes. Her strong frangipane perfume mingled with the cigarette smoke. Tall and thin, she was so striking and proud-looking that everyone noticed her and stared a while, despite themselves. A posh Parisienne, Xavier thought, down for the day. She was the sort who might have been one of his mother's glamorous socialite friends. What on earth could she have to do with the bishop?

At that moment, a tramp shuffled into view: at least, that was what Xavier took him for. His jeans were too long for him and frayed where they dragged on the floor, and he had the jaundiced, emaciated appearance of a drug addict. Where the tables parted to make a passage-way to the door of the bar, he stopped, looked inside and waited. He was clean-shaven but had lost all his front teeth. How old was he, Xavier wondered? Fifty, perhaps, although he looked eighty. It was impossible to tell.

A minute or two later, the boss came to the door and beckoned the man into the bar. Turning his head discreetly to watch, Xavier saw that he sat on a stool, where he was given something to eat and drink.

Looking forward again, Xavier stared at the green cross above the pharmacy across the street. Why the hell had he come to Angers to witness the verdict in person? Why was he torturing himself? Soon enough the decision would be blasted throughout the nation on the midday news. The fact that his former boss was likely to be a paedophile, and had taken everyone in with his charm and charisma, was not Xavier's fault. Rationally, reasonably, this he knew. But in eschewing the Church politics he abhorred and focusing on the nitty-gritty of his parish work, he had been naïve; at best, negligent, perhaps, in not asking awkward questions. Did that make him complicit? One thing was certain: it was not just one man that had been on trial these past months, but the Church itself.

Deep in the marrow of his bones, Xavier sensed an institutional cover-up. There was something dank and fetid that festered like the creeping green-and-black mould in the dark corner of a cellar in his parents' house. The feeling made his skin crawl. It was a feeling that had dogged him all through his childhood with his father's never-ending political machinations; a sense that the adults were not telling the truth and life as it was being sold to him, was a con. When the chips were down, the Church was like all established institutions: with any whiff of scandal or wrong-doing, it circled the wagons and protected its own. Whichever way the verdict went that morning, Xavier knew that the problem went far deeper than the former bishop alone. What did that mean for Xavier and his future as a priest? Would he stick his head in the sand once again and continue to serve, hidden away in a quiet country parish, or was it time to get out?

And with that came thoughts of Laura: how when they lay together, the vicissitudes of life had dissolved into showers of gold in his mind, and how in their mutual softness there was strength and joy. He remembered the two of them aeroplaneing into the wind along the beach, whooping with joy; the smell of sea salt and lavender mingled in her hair; the rich winey taste of a Bolognese sauce that they had slurped together from a wooden spoon; and her feet, deformed with years of merciless training, which he had kissed, toe by toe. In that instant, the cogs of his mind jammed, reason stalling to silence in the face of the two irreconcilable opposites within him. He heard nothing – not the banter of the journalists on the tables in front of him, not the sound of traffic, nor the hiss of steam from the coffee machine in the bar. He could not breathe and was briefly paralysed with panic, but then the sun moved with the day, seeping into his shade, placing a warm hand gently on his shoulder, easing him back to reality.

A car horn honked, and in front of him the camera crew began to stir, standing up, stretching, lifting their heavy kit. Their movement triggered a ripple of response across the bar; people lifted their heads, looked at their watches or phones, folded down their laptops and called for the bill.

'Gotta go!' a journalist shouted down his phone. 'Time to get the show on the road.'

Xavier watched as one by one the customers in the café drifted off down the road, until only he and the emaciated drug addict with no front teeth were left. As the tables were vacated, the man had come outside to sit in the sun. Xavier buttoned up his shirt collar and put on his tie; the act of doing this somehow made him feel a little more in control. Going into the bar to pay his bill, he offered to pay the other man's too, but the boss just smiled and waved his hand.

'Thank you, Monsieur, but it's not necessary. For those in need, it's on the house. Poor guy has been coming every day throughout that trial, but we don't ask.'

***

'It's your lucky day, Monsieur,' the usher quipped to Xavier at the door to the main courtroom where the trial had been heard. He pointed him to the last few available seats. Xavier sat at the back, three seats in from the aisle, his last-minute arrival causing a small ripple as people stood or twisted their knees to one side to let him pass.

Before him, the packed room appeared to undulate like a gentle sea, heads bobbing, small eddies spreading and lapping as lawyers and court officers moved about, heads together, consulting, whispering, gesturing, nodding about this and that. The expressions on all their faces was one of professional routine, affected boredom – but tinged with self-importance and nervous anticipation, for all the eyes in the room were on them, and this was a trial which had attracted huge publicity both within France and abroad. Although the evidence given against the former bishop had been compelling, the defence had been robust, and no one could be quite sure which way the verdict would go. But a conviction that day would be like throwing a bomb into the heart of the institution of the Church.

Xavier noticed the glamorous woman from the café, head held high, sitting at the front of the room. Two rows in front of him to the left was the toothless man whose bill he had tried to pay; shoulders hunched, he leaned forward with head down and might almost have been at prayer. Xavier scanned the rows of heads in front of him for people he knew – fellow priests or representatives of the Church – but recognised no one.

'All rise,' an usher called, and there was a scraping of chairs and benches and an outbreak of coughing. The President of the court, a diminutive grey-haired lady dressed in red robes, processed in, accompanied by her two fellow judges, in black, and six solemn-faced jurors. Somewhere below the floor, to the left, a metal door clanged. There was a brief jangle of keys, then the former bishop strode into the court, flanked by two guards. Everyone stared. He was a tall man but he stood taller that day, proud as a peacock, as if he were enjoying a moment of glory. He wore an expensive-looking navy suit and blue shirt which made him look more like a successful businessman than a priest. He was a leader; begrudgingly, Xavier had to give him that. He had always commanded with the sheer power of his presence, and he was doing the same this morning. All eyes were on him, admiring, fearing, worshipping… despising? Slowly, his large brown eyes roved around the court, passing methodically from row to row, but people looked down or turned their faces away.

Damn him! Damn him to hell!

It was as if a great balloon inflated in Xavier's chest, pressing against his ribs until he thought they would burst, pushing bile into his mouth. He recognised the old madness that once upon a time in his youth had led him to nearly murder his best friend. Xavier swallowed hard to keep it in check. He wanted to leap up, to plunge his fist into the man's face, to overturn tables, to throw chairs, to pulverise everything around him. But in that instant the former bishop's soft brown eyes fell upon him and he smiled at Xavier, almost imperceptibly, as if giving a blessing. Xavier wanted to roar with rage. Instead he stared back with hatred and contempt, eyes spitting fire.

There was a loud thump followed by a crackling as the President adjusted her microphone, then began to speak. Everyone looked at her – but not Xavier, who refused to release the bishop from his gaze. Two rows in front, to the left, the down-and-out from the café dropped his head and crossed himself.

It all happened so quickly; each charge was read, each verdict given, the grave words pronounced, slowly and precisely, giving time for the lawyers and clerk to take notes. Name after name, charge after charge. Guilty, guilty and guilty again. There were gasps and even a ripple of applause, so that the President had to call for order. Still Xavier held the former bishop in his gaze, looking for a flicker of remorse, but there was none. Only at the very last moment when the guard hand-cuffed the prisoner's hands did Xavier see it: the black shadow of fear on the man's face.

After the judges and jurors had retired, there was an outbreak of clapping, cheering, hugging and kissing in the court. A smiling young female lawyer came over to speak to the man from the café. She put his arm around his shoulders, and as he turned towards her, his face was wet with tears. Xavier trembled with fury. Justice had been done, but it was too little, too late; it could never fully restore the lives of those middle-aged men whom the former bishop had abused as boys.

Xavier allowed himself to be carried out of the courtroom on the momentum of the crowd. Only when they reached the grand entrance hall did he manage to escape. Hastily removing his jacket and tie, he went into the men's room, locked himself in a toilet stall, and vomited into the bowl. Sweating, he leaned against the wooden partition wall, listening to the snippets of conversation from outside. Gradually, the chatter and banter died down as people moved on. When everyone was gone, he came out and washed his face and mouth with cold water. He was calm now, but numb, utterly used up.

Somehow, he found himself on the front steps of the courthouse under the grand Greco-Roman portico. The sun was in his eyes and he was momentarily disorientated by the flash of cameras and the clamour of the crowd. The press had gathered and various news conferences were under way, lawyers and witnesses standing on the steps, reading out statements, answering questions. Xavier turned away to leave by the right-hand side of the steps.

'Father Michael!' Out of the shadows, a man ambushed him from behind one of the pillars. Portly and balding, he wore a pink Ralph Lauren polo shirt and carefully pressed chinos. He might have been dressed for a day's golf, but his footwear betrayed him; the shiny black leather shoes of a priest. Xavier recognised Father Philippe, one of the men on the former bishop's staff. He had never been quite sure of the man's precise status, but every time he had attended diocesan meetings, Father Philippe had been there taking minutes.

'So good of you to come today. Much appreciated, I am sure.' Father Philippe proffered his hand.

Xavier flicked his own hand to dismiss the gesture, but he was dumbstruck. Did the man think he had come here today as a show of support? Did he think the Church administration in the diocese could carry on as before?

Father Philippe responded by smiling and opening his right arm as if to invite Xavier to walk with him.

Rolling his shoulders, Xavier rooted himself to the ground, blocking his way.

'So how's that little tapestry project of yours coming along? The new bishop is really looking forward to the inauguration,' Father Philippe wheedled.

Xavier had a vision of the newly appointed, ultra-conservative bishop. He saw the puffed-up, pompous young man, dressed in all his finery, processing down the nave of his little church, so loved by the people in Le Saut. He imagined the new bishop, shaking hands with the parishioners, giving blessings, holding babies, as if he were St. Peter reincarnate. Furthermore, it occurred to Xavier that the parish would have to stump up for the hospitality out of their own meagre budget, for bishops and their entourages expected to be entertained. In that moment, Xavier knew the Church would never change.

Again anger welled up in his chest, the pent-up fury at the gross betrayal of trust by the former bishop and, Xavier was sure, by the institution of the Church itself.

Grabbing the other man by the scruff of the pristine pink polo shirt, he pushed him up against the pillar. He drew back his fist, the right one that once upon a time had been infamous in the regiment. Taut and tight, it was ready to fly. God knew, he wanted to smash this weasel's smug face, to see him grovel in his own blood, to see him suffer, but at the last minute Xavier sighed, turned his head away and spat into the ground. Releasing the man with a token little shove, he turned on his heels and walked quickly down the stone steps, away from the courthouse.

***

Afterwards, Xavier was ravenous, as if at the end of an endurance hike. All he could think of was food. In a little supermarket he bought a baguette, a packet of brie, a litre of water and a punnet of early Spanish strawberries. Returning to the car, he cursed himself for not having parked it in the shade, for the day was unseasonably hot. On the radio that morning, the weather forecast had warned of thunder-storms of a ferocity rarely experienced even during the summer months. Putting on his sunglasses and opening all the car windows, Xavier left the city as quickly as he could.

Eschewing the fast inland toll road, he took the scenic route that ran along the banks of the river. There she was, timeless, majestic, ferocious and deadly, bountiful and kind, the Queen of French rivers, old lady Loire. She was dressed in all her finery that day, a ribbon of emerald blue fringed with soft white and pink blossoms of lace. It was as if the river were keeping Xavier quiet company all the way.

After a while, he found a lay-by and stopped the car. Taking his lunch and a packet of emergency cigarettes from the glovebox, he made his way down to the river's edge and sat down under the trees. He ate lunch, breaking great hunks of bread and cheese with his hands, munching slowly, relishing the old familiar tastes. They reminded him of picnics with Mémé on the Île de Ré when he was a boy. In that moment, food had never tasted so good.

When he had eaten his fill, he leaned back against a tree trunk. Lighting a cigarette, he watched the sunlight and breeze playing across the surface of the river, drawing great fans of shimmering ripples. On the far side the current was strong, but on the side nearer him a narrow section of water meandered past a sandbank. Raising his head, he exhaled long breaths of smoke and watched them filter upwards through the blue gaps between the leaves in the canopy above him. Around him, the insects hummed and the birds sang, and in the shallows to his left a moorhen shepherded her brood of softly tweeting new-born chicks. Gradually Xavier's eyelids drooped, and he lay down on the ground; he would take a short snooze, just a while, he thought, why not?

The moment was effortless when it came. Somewhere in the shadowland between dream and reality, the decision that had been troubling Xavier's conscience for so long was made. When he awoke some two hours later, his mind was crystal clear. He felt as if he had slept a hundred years and had been born anew. All his worry and doubt had disappeared like the morning mist, and he knew what he must do.

CHAPTER 27

Late that afternoon, Xavier washed and changed, and went to see Laura at The House at the Foot of the Church. He walked bold as brass through the centre of the village, carrying a huge bunch of flowers, and did not give a damn who saw him.

Céline, La Folle Anglaise and the lady at the baker's watched him pass, and remarked upon it.

For her part, Laura stood at her bedroom window, smoking. Like her lover, she had relapsed that day, falling back on her old habit. Her hands trembled. Two miserly seconds – that was all it had taken to shatter her year of peace. That morning, for the first time in ages, she had logged on to her Hotmail account. Only two people in the world had that address: her broker in Rotterdam and the forger. There it had been: an email from the forger in Canada. It had been waiting ominously in her inbox for months without her knowing. It contained just one symbol, the simple two-stroke character for 'knife' that even a two-year-old could write; a warning, and no mistake. Laura inhaled deeply, holding the smoke in her lungs, trying to think. She exhaled long and slowly, trying to blow the smoke to the top of the church spire as if it might take her troubles with it. But she had run out of time. Her husband was coming for her. She had been happy hidden away in Le Saut; for the first time in her life, she had felt safe and free. But she had always known it was a beautiful dream that could not last, and now it was over.

Behind her in the main bedroom, the boxes were already packed, filled with the antiques and pretty things she had acquired for the house: the blue-and-white wash jug, the lace curtain runners so typical of the region, the set of English teacups decorated with pink roses, and Emilie, the porcelain-faced doll. But what an idiot Laura had been! She ought to leave now, abandoning everything, but needed just two more days to finish up; what harm could it do? And surely he would never find her, buried away in rural France? The storage company was due to come tomorrow afternoon to pick up the boxes, and she was expecting Wilhelm's trusted courier from Rotterdam to collect the painting first thing in the morning.

Of all her precious things, the picture of the old lady at prayer was the one she found most difficult to part with. It brought her closer to her mother and to something that only now was she beginning to comprehend, something she had experienced as a small child with her parents in their one-roomed apartment in Tianjin, a touchstone she had once possessed but which was long lost. She smelt incense and felt a sense of openness, rising to a clear blue sky. Such paradoxical emotions, Laura thought, for someone who did not believe in God. But her beloved painting must now be sold. It would disappear in the way of the other originals, and Laura would never see it again. Most likely it would end up on some drug baron's wall; for some reason, she imagined it hanging in a hacienda, surrounded by chattering monkeys in a jungle in South America.

Laura's plan was the usual one, tried and tested ever since she had fallen into the illicit business. Wilhelm would store the painting in his warehouse at the shipping port, let it lie there a little longer until they judged the time was right, and then it would be liquidated. That was his way of describing the murky process whereby he would put the original, highly-valued, painting on the international art black market and sell it at a hefty profit, one in which he, Laura and the forger all shared.

Stubbing out her cigarette in the ashtray on the window-sill, she put her head out and looked up and along the eaves and towards the rocky hill where it met the house walls. No sign of the swallows. She smiled at the thought of how they had kept her happy company the previous spring and summer. They had arrived about the same time she had, nesting in the crevices along the hill, pattering and tweeting along the eaves then darting out into the sunshine with a sharp whoosh of wings. Looking out across the cherry blossom, she knew it would be folly to try to settle down anywhere, ever again. Her fate was to wander the world. Only death could free her; either her own or her husband's, whichever came first.

Down in the kitchen, Boris barked. Then the gate clicked and Xavier came into the yard, his face half-hidden behind a massive spray of pink and purple flowers.

With one beat, Laura's heart leapt for joy, then sank to the depths with the next. What to do? Her living room was in disarray. If he came in there, he would see that she was leaving. She could not bear an emotional farewell, yet she could not turn him away. Making a snap decision, she hurried downstairs. She would meet him outside.

The moment she opened the kitchen door, he tumbled into the room, bringing with him sunshine and joy. He looked different, serene, years younger, as if a huge burden had been lifted from him.

'Fabulous news about the convictions. I saw it on the news.' Laura forced herself to sound natural. 'We should celebrate, perhaps?' She was unsure of the protocol in such circumstances and understood that Xavier had been struggling with his conscience for many years. In truth, she wanted to throw her arms around him and cover his funny, round face in kisses. But if she did that, she would burst into tears and reveal herself.

There was an awkward silence. Xavier looked disorientated, as if he did not comprehend what she said.

Laura waited for him to give her the flowers, but he did not. Perhaps she had misunderstood, and they were not for her at all?

'I've tidied up the kitchen, put some things away,' she said pre-emptively, thinking he might have noticed that the kitchen looked bare. But he just blinked and shook his head in confusion. He dithered from foot to foot, then all of a sudden went down on one knee, grabbed her hand and held up the flowers.

'Laura de Silva, I love you. Will you marry me?'

Laura's mind stalled. There were no words, not in French, not in Mandarin nor in Shanghainese, not in English. She was mute.

She must have looked funny, because he laughed and shrugged awkwardly. 'I've never done this before.' His face glowed with happiness like a small child's at Chinese New Year. Then slowly, agonisingly slowly, for it killed her to do so, Laura pulled her hand away. She might as well have kicked him in the stomach.

'I'm sorry,' he said, scrambling to his feet. 'Stupid of me to spring it on you like this. Sit down, sit down, please!' He gestured to the kitchen table, but Laura stood stock-still.

Reeling against the kitchen island behind him, Xavier put the flowers down.

'The thing is, I have renounced my holy orders. I am no longer a priest. I emailed my resignation this afternoon.'

It took a few seconds for Laura to understand what he was saying: that he was now free to marry.

'You should not have done that for me.' Laura found a voice, but it was not her own. It was as if someone else were speaking for her. 'I told you not to do that.'

'I did it, because it is the right thing to do. It's been a long time coming. Today was the final straw, the trigger for my decision. I know now that I cannot continue within the Church. There are other ways to live a good and true life. Laura, you have made me realise that.'

Laura hesitated. She could not lie to this man, whom she loved with all her heart. She owed him the truth.

'You do not know me, not really.' She spoke heavily, as if dredging words from the bottom of a muddy well. Reaching out, she took his hand and led him to the kitchen table. They sat down opposite each other.

'I'm leaving,' she said bluntly.

'Leaving where?'

'Le Saut.'

Xavier blinked in confusion. 'When are you coming back?'

Laura sighed, leaving his question hanging in the air. She

tried to explain. 'Xavier, I'm not who you think I am. I am not a good person. My previous life was not nice and not kind. I don't want you or anyone here in Le Saut getting mixed up in that.'

She could see that her explanation had been in vain, as Xavier shook his head. 'We are always a mystery to ourselves. God knows, I am. But I know you, Laura, and I love you regardless. The past is the past. It's over and gone.'

Tears pricked at Laura's eyes, but she blinked them away. 'How do you think I afford to live like this?'

She did not wait for an answer. She could no longer deceive him, no longer lie to this man whom she loved with all her heart. She owed him the truth.

She spoke harshly in a staccato manner. 'I am a fraudster and a thief. I started with diamond jewellery, having replicas made of the pieces and replacing the originals with them which I then sold on.' Laura laughed. 'It was pin money, and very amateurish. Then I met an artist and a European black-market dealer, and we went into the fine art business, you might say. It was a far more sophisticated operation, with my job being to ensure the fake paintings had provenance. Sometimes I would replace originals with fakes; sometimes we would manufacture a fake with provenance. I was lucky. I got in early, just as the Chinese art market was opening to the West.' She shrugged. 'The painting of the woman at prayer that you so admire. It's the original. It's worth millions. I kept it out of self-indulgence. The person who thinks he owns the original has a fake hanging on his wall!'

Dog paws pattered on the kitchen tiles. Boris had been sitting quietly on his bed in the corner of the kitchen. Sensing the tension between the humans, he got up and came to them for reassurance, going first to Xavier, then to Laura, his brown eyes big and sad.

Looking down at the dog, Xavier stroked the top of his head. 'I think,' he said quietly, 'that you did what you had to do.'

Then he looked her straight in the eye. 'Laura, I have seen the scars on your back. Never on my life, will I allow anyone to hurt you ever again.' He spoke quickly, thoughts and plans tumbling out as words. 'We can move away. I will have to leave the parish now I have resigned. We can start a new life, together. We can be happy. I know it. I don't care what you might have done. I ask again, marry me!'

Laura stood and drew herself up to her full height. It took all her strength to hold herself together, all her years of ballet training, all her experience of dissembling to survive. She was acting, on the stage performing a villainous role, but it had to be done to keep everyone safe. She hardened her face.

'Xavier, I'm already married.'

She saw the shock of betrayal on his face, and it ripped her heart to shreds.

'My husband is a Chinese businessman, very powerful and well connected.' Laura gritted her teeth, putting all her energy into delivering the final wicked lines.

'It's best if we never see each other again. Please leave.'

Xavier floundered like a landed fish, gasping for air, and she wanted to hold him in her arms and make everything right. Boris whimpered. Xavier stood up, his face drained to a ghostly white. His jaw twitched; he hesitated a second, looked at her as if she were a cockroach, then turned and marched like a soldier to the door. He did not slam it. It clicked quietly on the latch, and Laura heard his footsteps crunch into the distance across the gravel.

She went down into the deepest, darkest depths of the cellar, where only the ghosts could hear, and screamed into the silence. The walls absorbed her cries, soaked up her tears. There was no echo.

CHAPTER 28

Xavier was not sure how he arrived on the Île de Ré or why he had come, except perhaps that he was returning home. After leaving The House at the Foot of the Church, his memory was a blank, and it was already dark when he found himself driving across the long bridge to the island. Beneath him the sea seethed pitch-black. At his house, the pine trees whispered in the wind. Xavier had the impression that they were gossiping about him. He slammed the car door to shut them up.

Despite some unseasonal warmth, the house was chill. Unlike the previous, joyful time when he had visited with Laura, he had not turned on the heating remotely. Going back to the car, he grabbed his duffle bag and some shopping from the boot; he realised now that he must have stopped at the supermarket on the way, but had no recollection of having done so. There was a portion of paella from the deli, a baguette, some ham, cheese, eggs, butter and milk. Shivering with shock and fatigue, he lit the fire in the sitting room and sat down cross-legged in front of it to warm himself. Resisting the temptation to open a bottle of wine, he ate the paella directly from its box but did not taste it. The flames writhed in the grate, hungry for the well-seasoned wood. Xavier fed them with strips of polystyrene from the takeaway box, watching each piece flare red to orange and disintegrate. Physically, he was sitting in Mémé's house, but he was dead to himself, his mind numb beyond reason or pain. His body existed but, in that moment, no more than that.

Sleep took Xavier reluctantly in the early hours. He awoke late the following morning, stiff and cold, lying on the sofa. His breath was rancid with garlic, and he smelt of the previous day's sweat and grime. Outside, the wind rattled the shutters, and when he opened them, the clatter of the old-fashioned metal catches startled him. Looking out, he saw no promise, no hope in the ominous, slate-grey sky, but he went to the bathroom, showered, shaved and cleaned his teeth. He looked at himself in the mirror: his normally sparkling blue eyes were dull, his cheeks puffy and tired. Who was this person who stared back? A common-place, balding, middle-aged man, worthless, useless, no one he recognised as himself.

Xavier was consumed by a wave of anger and confusion. He had no real regrets about leaving the Church, but what about Laura? He remembered her standing in her kitchen, her face hard as stone, her eyes dead, biting cold. She was looking at him as if he meant nothing to her, telling him to get out. Had he meant nothing to her? He had thought they were happy, but he felt now that he had just been her plaything.

In the kitchen, he ground beans to make coffee; the chestnut colour of them in his hands, the familiar whirr of the machine and the intoxicating smell reduced his anger a notch. He downed three cups, one after the other, and forced himself to eat a thickly buttered tartine slathered in strawberry jam. It tasted like cardboard. Then, tugging on his running shoes, he banged furiously out of the house.

Xavier set off at a run along the sandy path that ran parallel to the Atlantic coast. To his left, the leaves and branches of the pine copse groaned and rolled threateningly in the wind. After barely a minute, he emerged from the relative shelter of the trees and was hit by the gale blowing in from the Atlantic. Like an invasion force, great banks of black clouds were amassed all along the western horizon. The day was wild and dark. Xavier pushed himself into a sprint to counter the wind. He was running next to a desolate beach. The seaweed and detritus that had washed up was like a barricade of barbed wire, but it would never stop the storm. The waves roared and the wet salt spray carried on the air. He understood all too well the power of the Atlantic storms that hit the island. All sane people would be battening down their possessions and getting where they needed to be, for soon the bridge to the mainland might be closed. It was madness to be out in such weather, but he did not care.

Turning sharp left, he set off inland into the marshes. With the wind at his back, he flew along as if given wings. On and on he ran, his heart thumping, his feet drumming, the wind roaring in his ears. His chest burned, his muscles screamed, but as he ran, he laughed, welcoming the storm, the grim fury of which matched his own. He wanted it to beat him, to punish him, to obliterate his pain.

Xavier was a lone figure in a red sweat-shirt, lost among the vast expanse of grey fringed with white that was the salt marshes. There were no birds that day, no other signs of life. He ran and ran, even when he thought he could run no further. He knew the paths like the back of his hand; he crossed the narrow stone bridge where, when he was small, he had imagined the trolls lived, and the tumble-down shed with its broken red bicycle that had been left outside for as long as anyone could remember. That had been his favourite picnic spot with Mémé. Sitting in the shade, they would name the birds and imagine they were cast-aways on a desert island and it was there, in the shadow of the shed, that he had kissed Laura.

But that day, Xavier did not stop nor see any of this. On and on he went, into the wilderness. He was exhausted, dripping in sweat, and slowed to a walk. Eventually, deep in the middle of the marshes, he stopped. It was no place, a hole in nothingness, with no distinction between the land and the sky. He turned back to face the sea and let the wind lash his face. In the distance, thunder cracked, and it began to rain.

Lifting his face to the sky, Xavier howled and howled, a wild, primeval scream that roared from the depths of his soul. The wind whipped it away, scattering it far across the marshes, and eventually words formed.

'Why? Why! Why?'

But there was no one to hear Xavier's cries. He was lost, forsaken, utterly alone.

It was now raining hard, and he was soaked to the skin. Shivering, he turned and strolled into the thunder and wind. All the fight had gone out of him.

***

Xavier did not know how long he had been out on the marshes, but at dusk he found himself on the beach near the house. The mighty waves still hurled themselves onto the beach. Slowly, deliberately, putting one foot in front of the other, he walked towards them. He was a child again, and he was not afraid. Stopping at the water's edge, he raised his eyes to the sky. The lightning forked, opening the clouds, and he saw him, his childhood friend, his old beloved who was at the same time faceless and without form, high among the clouds. The Golden Boy was now old, with a long white beard, but his gentle eyes were just the same.

The angel raised his arm and spoke.

'Go now. Hurry. She needs you.'

The darkness raced in, reconquering the space where the Golden Boy had been. He was gone, and Xavier knew this would be the last time his friend would ever appear to him. But in that instant, his reason was restored. He was calm, his mind crystal clear as if he had awoken from a trance. Laura had not been herself yesterday when she had asked him to leave. She was dissembling. She had escaped a life of violence and abuse, but not completely; someone else still had power over her and was pulling her strings. She was sacrificing herself and their love because she had no choice. Something terrible was about to happen to Laura. He knew it, and he had to get to her before it was too late.

Fatigue and exhaustion vanished, and Xavier sprinted back to the house. He towelled himself down roughly and put on his cassock. He did not stop to pack, but jumped into the car, fastening his dog collar as he drove. The rain poured; the windscreen wipers whirred at triple speed but struggled to keep up with the torrent. Putting his foot down, Xavier raced headlong into the night.

Xavier's heart pounded. He recognised the old, bittersweet sensation of fight, of being under fire. It was now or never. Xavier hoped the bridge would be open and revved the accelerator. As he approached the bridge, he heard someone shout,

'You're a fucking idiot, Father!

'Was he entrusting his soul to God or the devil?'

It took all his strength to keep the car firmly under control. Nearly blinded by spray, the road surface was glassy black, treacherous with rain and he could barely see two metres in front.

Suddenly, a gust of wind picked up the car and tossed it to sharply to the right. Xavier felt himself falling, closed his eyes, and thought of Laura.

CHAPTER 29

'Boris, Boris! Where are you?' Laura shouted into the wind and rain. She locked the door for the last time, and posted the key into the letter box for the estate agent to pick up. The painting had been collected and she had just finished loading the minimum of personal possessions into the van. It was time to go, but where was the dog? He had been at her side barely half an hour ago.

Thunder boomed like cannons. Lightning cracked and split the sky, illuminating the church tower. Somewhere up the road, a shutter banged.

'Boris! *Boris!*' The wind whipped at the hood of Laura's raincoat and swallowed her desperate calls.

Should she leave without the dog, abandon him in France? The villagers would look after him. Perhaps it would be the better solution, for the animal had been happy here. Perhaps she should wait and leave in the morning… But no. Her time was up. The thought of abandoning her canine companion pained Laura, but her terror of her husband was too strong. He was near; her body was her barometer, and it knew. Her bones ached, her teeth chattered. Every muscle and fibre in her body had told her to leave that night, under the cover of the storm and not to delay.

Laura opened the front door of the van and reached for the torch lying on the driver's seat. She would scan the garden quickly one last time for Boris.

Suddenly, the van door slammed into her side, taking her breath away and knocking her off balance. Someone grabbed her from behind, ramming her head down viciously. She screamed, but her cries were muffled.

'Shut the fuck up, whore!'

She smelt him, all whisky and aftershave mingled with tobacco. It was him, her husband. He had found her.

Still pushing her down, he wrenched her arms back to tie them behind her back. She kicked out with all her strength, but he was a big man, well over six feet tall, and he wedged her legs into the corner of the van door using the door and his weight to constrain her. For a second, he yielded a fraction, and she resisted with all her might. Briefly, she managed to raise her head and scream, but her cries were lost in a boom of thunder.

Having secured her arms, he grabbed her by the throat. Choking was a method of torture that he enjoyed; on many occasions, she had thought he would kill her. This time, she knew, he would not stop at rape.

As he heaved her around to face him, she saw the pleasure in his eyes. The lightning flashed again somewhere away in the village, and Boris barked.

'Bitch!' he spat, and struck her hard in the face with his fist. She remembered no more.

***

There was the splatter of running water, and Laura tasted blood. She struggled to open her eyes, bright lights blinding her. She tried to move her arms and legs, but they were bound; she tried to call out, but could not move her mouth.

Gradually, consciousness returned. She was tied to a chair in the kitchen with her mouth taped up. Laura cranked her head to the right. The movement provoked a burst of stabbing silver shards. He had rolled up his shirt sleeves and was washing his hands in the kitchen sink. Had he come alone? Of course he had. Other cleaning jobs, as he called them, he gave to one of his henchmen, but when it came to her, he enjoyed it too much and always took his vengeance alone. He had his back to her and was scrubbing his nails and forearms meticulously, as if he were a surgeon preparing for an operation.

A mighty terror welled up inside Laura. She battled this way and that, but could only groan, and her legs were so tightly and expertly bound to the chair that she could get no leverage. Realising that struggle at this stage was futile, she quietened, waiting, shivering with fear, knowing she had no way out. He was rifling through her cupboards, banging the doors, one by one.

'Got any coffee? The food in France is shit, but the coffee is good. Doesn't look like it? Never mind.' He reached into his shirt pocket and drew out a packet of cigarettes. Slowly withdrawing one, he lit it and sucked long on it.

'Did you think you could outwit me, bitch? No one, I mean *no one*, gets away from me.' Another puff on his cigarette. He was taking his time. 'So where are they, the paintings and diamonds? The originals, not the fakes. Never mind. I've got you now, and I will get it out of you. You'll squeal like your Canadian artist friend before I'm done. I want back what is mine – all of it.' The corner of his mouth twitched in the way it did when he was angry, and Laura knew she had wounded his pride. 'Did you miss me? Must have done. You've got a French lover, I'm told – a priest. Have you no shame, whore?' Slowly, deliberately, he stubbed out his cigarette on the kitchen top. 'I've half a mind to take back what is mine, but you've gone and soiled yourself. My, how you've let yourself go!'

His punch came out of nowhere, winding her in the stomach, then a series of slaps, hard across her face. Outside, the wind howled. Laura heard Boris barking, and the front door slam. Again he punched her, winding her once more. She was losing consciousness again. Everything before her was distant and fuzzy…

Then came a terrifying sound: a wild snarling, like a lion. She saw Boris spring at her husband's throat. He tried to fend the dog off with his right arm, cursing in Shanghainese. There was a maelstrom of shouting and growling. The dog had the man on the floor and was locked onto his throat with his teeth as the two of them wrestled.

The last thing Laura was aware of was the flashing of something that looked like Madame Mini's pink, starry walking stick in the kitchen spotlights.

EPILOGUE: THE TAPESTRY TEACHER

So- there you have it - all our secrets! But wait, there are just a few more threads left to weave. Don't be so impatient! Everything in good time. What joy to breathe the sea air! Drink it in! It's so long since I had a holiday. Look – there, in front of the ferry, you can see the island, the Île de Ré. I've never been before, and I'm excited. Are you wondering why I'm going there? I'll tell you. I'm going to see Laura and Father Michael, or Xavier, as he is now. They moved to the island after the pandemic.

Ah – Covid, you say. Quite right, yes. It changed the landscape of so many lives, and ours in the village, too. Nothing was quite the same. We lost Henri Duguet, the café owner, and Old Santelli. Madame Rossignol caught the virus twice and survived, but died six months later of old age. There is no one left in the village who remembers the war.

And Xavier and Laura? Well, Laura is free. They are happy now. Xavier left the priesthood, and they married. They sold The House at the Foot of the Church and moved to the Île de Ré. The old place is owned now by a Dutch couple; they've given it a new lease of life. They run a bed and breakfast, and yoga retreats. No, they don't know the history of the house. It's better that way.

But you want to know what happened that night. You're in deep enough now. I'll tell you the truth – but remember, I swore you to secrecy.

Do I look like a murderer? I'll let you judge.

That night of the storm, I was just locking up the studio when I noticed Boris. I thought he was just having a foray into the village, but he would not leave me alone, barking and pulling at my skirt. Sensing that something was wrong, I grabbed my walking stick and followed him back down the hill to the House at the Foot of the Church. It was a foul night and the whole village was shuttered up against the weather. At the house, I found the front door open and saw lights on in the kitchen. Laura's van also had the door open, which I thought odd.

There was a man in the kitchen with Laura, and he was beating her.

All at once I was a child again, at home witnessing my father abusing my mother. As a girl I had been powerless to stop it, but that night I was possessed by a demonic rage. Boris, too, played his part, wrestling the man down to the floor and mauling him terribly around the neck and throat while I lifted my stick and hit his head again and again with the handle. The dog fought with the strength of a hundred lions. I did not stop him.

We did not stop until Xavier stayed my hand from behind and took Boris by the collar.

'Enough, Madame Mini, enough.'

And all of a sudden, the house was quiet while the man gushed blood on the floor. It was carnage. His throat had been ripped out. He choked to death right there in front of our eyes…

Give me a minute. It's a hard story to tell.

Father Michael took charge, cool as a cucumber, releasing Laura from her bonds and covering the man up with a blanket. After that, he sent Laura home with me. I don't know what he did with the body, but I do know that men of the Legion came in the early hours of the morning. They have their own code, their own ways, their own justice. Xavier never said anything about it, other than that the intruder would never trouble Laura again. As for Boris, the following morning Xavier took him up onto the hill for a walk and shot him.

So now you know it all. We're nearly there now. Xavier and Laura said they'd meet us off the boat. There they are, waving! Xavier has his arm around Laura. Don't they look happy! You will get to meet them at last. They tell me that you're invited for dinner? Good. You can ask Xavier himself if he still has faith. But look there, between the sea and sky. It's almost as if you can see angels.'

Fin

ABOUT THE AUTHOR

Rhiannon Jenkins Tsang is a British author whose work focuses on cultural and historical fault lines and has strong international themes. Rhiannon was born in Yorkshire and has studied, lived and worked in Europe and Asia. She read Oriental Studies (Chinese) at Oxford and speaks Mandarin and Cantonese. Rhiannon lives in a former farmhouse in rural England with her family.

Novels:

The Woman Who Lost China, Open Books 2013

The Last Vicereine, Penguin Random House 2017

The Dream That Held Us, Bunny Publishing 2021

Short Story Anthology:

Hong Kong Noir, Akashic Books 2019

www.ingramcontent.com/pod-product-compliance
Ingram Content Group UK Ltd.
Pitfield, Milton Keynes, MK11 3LW, UK
UKHW042033041025
463617UK00002B/26